BIG TROUBLE

Clint swung around to face the door. "Big Joe Gritts," he hissed. "How'd you get out of prison?"

Gritts smiled through tobacco-stained horse teeth. "You and me," he said, "we can go to the dance later. Right now, the reward for Blackstone and his boys interests me."

"I've got a score to settle myself with Harry Blackstone," Clint said. "You'd best keep a long, long way out of my sight."

"It's a free country, and this ain't your town like it was down in Texas. You ain't spit here, Adams. And if you try and stop me again, I'll squash you like a damn dirty bug."

Also in THE GUNSMITH series

MACKLIN'S WOMEN
THE CHINESE GUNMAN
THE WOMAN HUNT
THE GUNS OF ABILENE
THREE GUNS FOR GLORY
LEADTOWN
THE LONGHORN WAR
QUANAH'S REVENGE
HEAVYWEIGHT GUN
NEW ORLEANS FIRE
THE PONDEROSA WAR
TROUBLE RIDES A FAST HORSE
DYNAMITE JUSTICE
THE POSSE
NIGHT OF THE GILA
THE BOUNTY WOMEN
BLACK PEARL SALOON
GUNDOWN IN PARADISE
KING OF THE BORDER
THE EL PASO SALT WAR
THE TEN PINES KILLER
HELL WITH A PISTOL
THE WYOMING CATTLE KILL
THE GOLDEN HORSEMAN
THE SCARLET GUN
NAVAHO DEVIL
WILD BILL'S GHOST
THE MINER'S SHOWDOWN
ARCHER'S REVENGE
SHOWDOWN IN RATON
WHEN LEGENDS MEET
DESERT HELL
THE DIAMOND GUN
DENVER DUO
HELL ON WHEELS
THE LEGEND MAKER
WALKING DEAD MAN
CROSSFIRE MOUNTAIN
THE DEADLY HEALER
THE TRAIL DRIVE WAR
GERONIMO'S TRAIL
THE COMSTOCK GOLD FRAUD
BOOMTOWN KILLER
TEXAS TRACKDOWN

THE FAST DRAW LEAGUE
SHOWDOWN IN RIO MALO
OUTLAW TRAIL
HOMESTEADER GUNS
FIVE CARD DEATH
TRAILDRIVE TO MONTANA
TRIAL BY FIRE
THE OLD WHISTLER GANG
DAUGHTER OF GOLD
APACHE GOLD
PLAINS MURDER
DEADLY MEMORIES
THE NEVADA TIMBER WAR
NEW MEXICO SHOWDOWN
BARBED WIRE AND BULLETS
DEATH EXPRESS
WHEN LEGENDS DIE
SIX-GUN JUSTICE
MUSTANG HUNTERS
TEXAS RANSOM
VENGEANCE TOWN
WINNER TAKE ALL
MESSAGE FROM A DEAD MAN
RIDE FOR VENGEANCE
THE TAKERSVILLE SHOOT
BLOOD ON THE LAND
SIX-GUN SHOWDOWN
MISSISSIPPI MASSACRE
THE ARIZONA TRIANGLE
BROTHERS OF THE GUN
THE STAGECOACH THIEVES
JUDGMENT AT FIRECREEK
DEAD MAN'S JURY
HANDS OF THE STRANGLER
NEVADA DEATH TRAP
WAGON TRAIN TO HELL
RIDE FOR REVENGE
DEAD RINGER
TRAIL OF THE ASSASSIN
SHOOT-OUT AT CROSSFORK
BUCKSKIN'S TRAIL
HELLDORADO
THE HANGING JUDGE

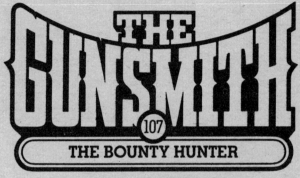

THE GUNSMITH

107

THE BOUNTY HUNTER

J. R. ROBERTS

J

JOVE BOOKS, NEW YORK

THE BOUNTY HUNTER

A Jove Book/published by arrangement with
the author

PRINTING HISTORY
Jove edition/November 1990

ISBN: 0-515-10447-7

Jove Books are published by The Berkley Publishing Group,
200 Madison Avenue, New York, New York 10016.
The name ''Jove'' and the ''J'' logo
are trademarks belonging to Jove Publications, Inc.

PRINTED IN THE UNITED STATES OF AMERICA

10 9 8 7 6 5 4 3 2 1

ONE

The Gunsmith halted before the plate-glass window of the largest emporium in Carson City, Nevada, and swept off his black Stetson to study his reflection before he called upon Miss Lucinda Butler. Clint Adams did not consider himself a handsome man, though women seemed to find him very attractive, despite the thin scar across his left cheek. He was slightly taller than average, slender and lean faced. His black hair was straight and thick and he combed it with his fingers, then replaced the Stetson, setting it carefully at just the right angle. His coat and trousers were black, his shirt new and white, stiffly starched. He wore his six-gun prominently, though not tied down in the manner of a professional gunfighter.

"She'll think you handsome enough," a matronly woman by the name of Agnes Moore said with a smile. "In fact, if I were twenty years younger, I'd sure cast my fishing net in your direction."

Clint chuckled. Agnes owned a millinery store just up the street, and Clint had met her one afternoon when shopping for a present for Miss Butler's twenty-first birthday. They had formed a liking for each other, and now, every time Clint walked down Carson City's main street, he enjoyed popping in on Agnes.

His sudden appearance in a ladies' store always caused a

great stir among Agnes's customers, mostly older respectable ladies who thought it titillating to be in the company of a famous exsheriff and gunfighter—and a crushingly handsome one, besides!

"You aren't going to go and get yourself married, are you?" Agnes asked with a frown.

"Married?" Clint shook his head. "Not hardly, ma'am! I'm just looking to enjoy the company of a beautiful lady, and if you weren't already married, I'd be after knocking on your door."

Agnes threw her head back and laughed with amusement. "Ha! You must have some Irish in your blood, Mr. Adams, because you sure can throw the blarney around. But you watch out for Miss Lucinda. If you're not careful, she'll put a ring through your nose and make you put a ring on her finger."

"I'm a committed bachelor," Clint said.

"Miss Lucinda could change all that," Agnes said, only half teasing now. "She's pretty, smart, and charming, and her father, being Carson City's most prominent and successful banker, is rich. The young man who catches her for a prize will be fortunate indeed. Even without a dime to her name, she'd be the best catch in western Nevada. You watch out now."

"I will," Clint said, tipping his hat as Agnes waddled on toward the Bank of Carson City to make her daily deposits.

Clint shook his head. He had been living in this town for about two months now, after opening his own little gunsmith shop. Business was good, and he liked the town and its people. Carson City rested at the eastern base of the Sierra Nevada Mountains at an elevation of five thousand feet. To the east stretched the great high-desert plateaus of Nevada. To the north was Washoe Lake and then Reno, and up on the Comstock Lode, Virginia City, Silver City, and Gold Hill were booming.

In Carson City, if a man got too warm in the summer, he

could ride up to Lake Tahoe and swim in water cold enough to freeze his gonads off or just camp for a few weeks in the whispering pines. And if he became too cold in the winter, he could always ride south toward Death Valley, where it was a perpetual summer.

"Afternoon, Mr. Adams," the town saddlemaker called as he swept out his store.

"Afternoon," Clint said, passing along the boardwalk, greeting and being greeted by merchants and citizens alike.

Yes sir, the Gunsmith liked this town. Being a legitimate merchant with his own little shop made him feel right at home. And while he could have more business up on the booming Comstock Lode, where gunfights and brawls were a daily occurrence, Clint preferred the tranquillity of the capital of Nevada. Money, after all, wasn't everything in life. A man who worked too hard tended to miss smelling the roses or a girl like Lucinda's perfume.

Clint stopped at the corner across from the high-domed capitol building. He was supposed to meet Lucinda here at noon, but he was fifteen minutes early. No problem. The capitol grounds were shady with large trees, and he could stroll around the huge sandstone state buildings for a few minutes and enjoy the day. After he and Lucinda had lunch, they would rent a carriage and drive up to Virginia City to visit friends, whom they would accompany to Piper's Opera House for a Shakespearean play, *The Taming of the Shrew*.

Clint could think of other entertainment that he'd have preferred to engage in with Lucinda. He had managed so far to make some physical advances during their courtship, but she was playing very hard to get. Clint suspected that, even though the girl was twenty-one, she was still a virgin and intended to remain in that state of innocence.

The Gunsmith smiled. The greater the challenge, the sweeter

the victory. He strolled around the capitol grounds, admiring the trees and watching the red and gray squirrels overhead jump and chatter in the tall branches.

"Hello there, Mr. Adams!" a dignified man in a gray suit said as he emerged from the capitol building. "I thought you and Lucinda were on your way up to Virginia City."

Clint turned and saw Lucinda's father coming toward him with an outstretched hand. They shook hands warmly, and Clint was once again reminded that Mr. Butler had not always been so friendly. Indeed, he had been chill to the Gunsmith at first. But Clint could not have been a sheriff for so many years without learning a few things about gaining a man's cooperation, and after a few weeks, he'd won Mr. Butler's friendship.

"Your daughter had a last-minute appointment to keep, so we are going up after lunch."

Mr. Butler had a folded newspaper under his arm, and he pulled it out with a frown. "The *Carson City Appeal* reports that there was another stagecoach robbery just down Six Mile Canyon from Gold Hill. That's the road you'll be going up. You watch out for my daughter's safety, Mr. Adams. And when you arrive at her uncle's house, make sure that she delivers my greeting."

"I will." Lucinda would be staying at her uncle's home in Virginia City, but Clint had met the man and he had hopes of figuring out some way to stay close, just in case Lucinda's resistance began to weaken after the play and a little champagne.

Mr. Butler started to pass. "Got to get back to the bank," he said. "I sure hope that the Blackstone Gang is caught and brought to justice—and soon. They figure that this one gang has pulled off no less than ten robberies and holdups in the last seven weeks! They took the Bank of Virginia City last month for seven thousand dollars. I tell you, it's a good thing we don't carry the kind of money in our vault that they do up on the Comstock. If we did, I'd be worried!"

"They'll catch those boys," Clint promised. "I've been reading about them, too. There's a United States marshal and a number of other lawmen that are doing everything they can to trap that gang. Sooner or later Blackstone will walk into a trap, and then his days of lawlessness will be over."

The banker hesitated. "You know, there's a two-thousand-dollar reward for the capture of Blackstone, and the rewards for the capture of his men must total another three thousand. Five thousand dollars is a lot of money. You ever think of maybe . . . "

"No," Clint said, anticipating the question. "I was a sheriff but never a bounty hunter, except on a few occasions when someone killed or hurt a friend of mine. Bounty hunting is a dirty business, especially when the authorities pay a reward dead or alive."

"Which the authorities are, in this case."

"Yes," Clint said. "That kind of reward pulls a lot of fools out of the woodwork, and I've seen inexperienced men call themselves bounty hunters when they had no business hunting anything bigger than groundchucks. They either get themselves shot or they shoot some innocent victim, or they even start shooting each other to whittle down the competition."

"It does sound like a bad business," Mr. Butler said. "Well, I was just curious. A man like yourself, with your reputation and experience—I just thought he might have a strong pull to jump into that game as the reward climbs week after week. Every time that Harry Blackstone and his gang pull off another cold-blooded robbery and killing, they up the ante several thousand dollars."

"Not interested."

The banker almost looked disappointed. "Well, I've got to go now. Again, take good care of my daughter and enjoy the play. I wish I was going along with you, but I've got to mind my own store, even if some men don't."

Clint caught the hint of reproach in the banker's voice. He was beginning to think of Clint as a potential son-in-law and he wanted Clint to start acting more like a businessman. Clint understood that. If he had a daughter, he'd want her to marry a successful, hardworking young man who had an eye for business and the future.

"Maybe some time we can discuss a business loan," the banker said. "If you had more capital, you might expand. Start carrying other goods and—"

"Thanks," Clint said, cutting the banker off with a smile, "but I'm a gunsmith, and I don't want to go into 'other' goods. Appreciate the offer anyway."

Mr. Butler was disappointed. "You either grow in business or you die, Clint. I'm just trying to make sure that you grow."

"Much obliged," Clint said, seeing Lucinda appear up the street. "And don't you worry: I'll take good care of your daughter."

"I know that. There's not a man in Nevada more capable of handling trouble than you, Clint."

The banker refolded his paper and walked on with a slight frown on his face. Maybe he was troubled by the lack of Clint's ambition to expand his business or maybe he was worried about the Blackstone Gang. Either way, the moment Clint saw Lucinda, he didn't care.

She was wearing a long white dress trimmed in yellow, and her bonnet was the one that Agnes had displayed in her millinery-store window.

Clint inhaled deeply. The sun was shining and the thin, high-desert air was sweet in the spring. He found it enjoyable just to watch Lucinda as she walked across the capitol grounds toward him, a smile on her pretty lips and a sway to her pretty hips.

Damn she was pretty! She had long yellow hair and bright

blue eyes. Clint had never seen her in anything tight fitting, but he would bet his bedroll that she was built like a love goddess. She had long legs and was tall for a woman—maybe five-eight—slender in the waist and full in just the right places. She made him lustful and, at the same time, aware that a young woman like Lucinda might even be worth the trials of marriage.

When she saw Clint she waved, and her step quickened in anticipation as Clint went to meet her. Ordinarily he would have taken her hands and said something clever, but she looked so damned luscious this morning that he could not help himself, so he swooped her up in his arms and kissed her full and passionately, right in front of the capitol and everyone who watched.

Lucinda struggled for a moment, then melted in his embrace. She wrapped her arms around his neck and her mouth was hungry for his. He swore he could feel her heart pounding through their clothing.

"My!" she panted when they broke apart. "If my father hears of this, he'll be furious. And someone is bound to start gossiping."

"Let them gossip," Clint said, looking into her eyes, which were bluer than the waters of Lake Tahoe but much, much warmer. "Today is ours to enjoy."

"And what about tonight?" she asked, a slight smile forming on her lips.

"You mean the play and dinner, of course."

"Of course. What else?"

Clint knew that she was baiting him. Lucinda might or might not be a virgin, but she was definitely a little bit of a tease. She was also fully aware of the effect she had on a man, and she exploited her charms without shame or reservation.

"I was thinking," Clint said, "that maybe it wouldn't be nice to put your dear old uncle to any inconvenience, and I know a nice hotel where we could . . . "

She laughed. "Think again, Clint. Do you really imagine that my father won't check to make sure I stayed with my uncle while you stayed elsewhere?"

"I guess that is a little naive, huh?"

"Very," Lucinda said, slipping her arm through his. "So whatever little designs you may have on me for tonight, I'd put them right out of my mind."

"You can't blame a red-blooded man for hoping," he said.

Lucinda laughed, and the sound of it was like crystal wind chimes, melodic and beautiful.

"So," she said, as they came back upon the street, "where shall we eat?"

There were at least four restaurants and cafes in town and they were all fairly good. "You choose," he said, hoping she did not select one of the more expensive, because the night's entertainment was probably going to cost him a bundle.

"Let's have something simple and inexpensive," she said, "since we are going to feast tonight. Which, by the way, I insist on paying for."

"You can't do that!"

She squeezed his arm. "Of course I can! You're paying for the play, I'm paying for our dinner. That's only fair, considering that I'm a spoiled little rich girl."

Clint laughed outright. "You're the only rich girl I ever met who wasn't spoiled," he said—meaning it because it was true. Lucinda enjoyed nice things, but the thing that was most special about her was that she did not make a show of having money or trying to find a man who also had money. She seemed entirely oblivious to class or social standings. As the only child of a widower banker, she would someday inherit a small fortune and she could have had any man in the state, but she had taken to Clint. And every time he thought about that fact, it made him proud as could be.

"Now that we've settled the finances," she was saying as

they walked arm in arm up the boardwalk, "I was thinking that . . . "

An alarm sounded in Clint's brain as his eyes happened to fasten on a group of six horses being held in front of the Bank of Carson City. The man who held their reins wore a gun tied down low in his hip and a hat pulled down even lower over his forehead.

Clint stopped dead in his tracks. He'd been a lawman enough years to recognize that something was very wrong in the street up ahead.

"What's wrong?"

Clint gently pushed the girl away from him toward a side alley. "I got a feeling," he said, reaching for his six-gun. "Just stay off the street. It may be nothing, but . . . "

The front door of the bank suddenly opened, and Clint saw five men hurry out. Despite the fact that the weather was mild and sunny, they were all wearing heavy dusters, and from the bulges Clint saw under their coats, he was ninety-nine percent certain that each man was carrying a lot of stolen cash.

"Hey!" he shouted, running forward with his gun in his fist.

The five men saw him all at the same time and they went for their guns. Clint put a bullet through one man and dove for cover as a hail of lead filled the air.

No doubt about it, he thought. I'd better get reinforcements in a hurry, or I've bitten off more than I can chew.

Clint dared to lift his head over the lip of the watering trough just in time to see a big man that fit the description of Harry Blackstone fire at him.

Clint ducked, but the bullet ate threw the wooden trough, sending splinters into his face.

"Clint!"

He twisted around to see Lucinda running to his aid.

"No!" Clint shouted, jumping to his feet and trying to reach the girl and knock her down before she was felled by a bullet.

Clint tackled Lucinda, then covered her with his body as bullets screamed across the street. The Blackstone Gang jumped onto their horses and came storming down the street, firing at anything that moved. As they passed Clint, who was trying to shield the banker's daughter with his body, Harry Blackstone barked a laugh and unleashed two bullets from a range of not more than twenty feet.

Clint felt the first slug punch him in the side and break through his ribs. He grunted with pain and then tried to twist around and fire up at the bank robbers.

Blackstone emptied his gun at Clint, and even though he was astride a racing horse, a second bullet creased Clint's skull, knocking his Stetson into the air.

The six-gun dropped from Clint's fist and he grabbed at his head as a firestorm erupted behind his eyes.

"Clint!" Lucinda screamed.

He tried to answer her, but his voice sounded as if it were being swept away in a Texas tornado. Then he dropped into the eye of the storm and went spinning off into oblivion.

TWO

"Clint!" Lucinda screamed as she rolled him over, only to realize that he'd been shot in the head and the side. "Oh, Clint, no!"

Lucinda raised her head and looked wildly around. "Doctor! Someone find Doctor Olms!"

No one heard her at first. The Blackstone Gang was still racing out of town and everyone was firing at them, though their shots were wild and more a danger to themselves than to the vicious outlaws who had just robbed their bank.

When the gang had disappeared around a corner, people turned to see Lucinda holding the unconscious Clint Adams in her arms, and their first impression was that the famous gunman had been killed. He was covered with blood. The head wound had leaked all over Lucinda's white dress and the wound in Clint's side was just as bad.

"Doctor!" she cried. "Get a doctor!"

Agnes Moore staggered out of the bank. "Help," she cried weakly, "someone please help!"

Lucinda twisted around to see Agnes with blood running down her cheek. Then the dear old woman pitched forward into the street as men raced to her side and others hurried into the bank.

Doctor Olms arrived on the run. He was in his sixties and no longer spry, but he was competent and it took him less than ten seconds to examine Clint's wounds and shout, "Get this man to my office!"

Several merchants grabbed Clint and carried him away as the doctor rushed to Agnes. He examined her for a minute and then shouted, "Take her to my office as well. Hurry!"

One of the bank clerks staggered out onto the boardwalk and shouted, "Doc! It's Mr. Butler! He's . . . he's dead!"

"No!" Lucinda cried, jumping to her feet and racing through the crowd into her father's bank.

Someone caught her in the lobby and said, "I don't think it would be a good idea if you went into your father's office, Miss Lucinda. It ain't pretty."

"Let go of me!" She broke free and bolted around the teller's cage into her father's office.

He was lying facedown in a pool of blood, and she almost fainted. Her hand closed over her mouth and stifled a scream. Lucinda fell to her knees sobbing. She rolled her father over to hug him, and when she saw the way his throat had been cut, she did scream. And she kept screaming until the sheriff arrived and the shocked onlookers could pull her out of her father's office and outside.

"What are we going to do with her!" a man shouted.

Doctor Olms could not help the banker, so he came outside and said, "Let's get her to my office. I've got some opium. I don't like to use it, but in a case like this it might keep her from losing her mind. She should never have been allowed to see her father like that, goddamnit!"

"I tried to stop her," a man said, "but she was a wildcat!"

The doctor didn't want to hear excuses. "Anyone else hurt?"

"Two men that jumped out in the street and tried to stop the Blackstone Gang were gunned down. You can't do a thing for either one of them, Doc."

"The poor fools," the doctor said. "See if you can find our pickled mortician. Sober him up and tell him he's got work to do and he'd better by God get to it, or we'll run him the hell out of town for keeps this time."

"Yes sir," a man said as he hurried away to find the undertaker.

Doctor Jebediah Wilson Olms hurried into his office, his mind churning as he quickly reviewed the three cases that he would have to treat. Agnes Moore, the milliner, had obviously been pistol-whipped by some brutish sonofabitch who'd not cared a damn whether he crushed her skull or not. And although he had only examined her for a moment, Doctor Olms was sure that the woman was suffering from a severe concussion. She might recover; then again, she might have permanent brain damage. Or perhaps a life-threatening blood clot on the brain would kill her.

Doctor Olms had received his medical training at the finest medical school in the country, one near New York City. But that had been twenty-six years before, and although he had learned a great deal since coming west to practice medicine, he was a man who knew his limitations, and he was no brain surgeon. If there was a clot on Agnes's brain, she would surely die.

Miss Lucinda was an entirely different concern. She had suffered extreme emotional trauma: first in being shielded by a man's bullet-riddled body—a man she was probably in love with—and then upon witnessing the horrible sight of her father lying in his own blood with his throat sliced open.

Doctor Olms had seen many brutal, fiendish killings in his years on the frontier but none so chilling as this. No doubt the banker had tried to call out in alarm, and to silence him permanently as well as to make an example for the others, Blackstone or one of his monsters had slit the man's throat and left him gagging in his own gore.

Doctor Olms wondered if the delicate and beautiful Lucinda's mind would be permanently unhinged by the sight of her father as he opened up his satchel and tore around inside it until he found two envelopes.

"Here," he said, ripping the envelopes open and pouring them in a glass. "Give Miss Butler these powders at once with water!"

A woman did as he ordered. "What are they?"

"Opium," the doctor snapped as he rushed over to his examining table and began to attend to the Gunsmith. Men were crowding around him, making the air close and jostling him, so Olms yelled, "Get of here! Everyone get out except the sheriff and—"

"The sheriff is forming a posse. He ain't here, Doc!" It was Mark Day, the owner of the town's biggest feed store. He was a good man, steady and sensible.

"All right, Mark, then you stay and run the rest out. I need some room and some quiet to work!"

He turned his attention back to Clint. His fingers probed Clint's skull, where a bullet had plowed through bone, then ricocheted off.

"It was probably one of those silver conches on his hatband," Mark said.

"Look," he added, raising Clint's hat from his side. "See this flattened silver conch? That's where Blackstone's bullet hit and then glanced."

"Huh," the doctor grunted. "Well, it didn't glance quite enough. But you're right—it probably saved his life."

The doctor next examined Clint's side. He ripped the Gunsmith's coat and vest away, then pulled up his ruined white shirt. The wound was ugly as sin, but it wasn't fatal.

"This man has more luck than a cat with nine lives," he said to the feed-store owner. "Two bullets, and neither one of them killed him."

"Those splinters in his face sure look nasty," Mark said.

"I'll pull them out as soon as I've taken care of the more

serious things," the doctor said, reaching for a pan. "Here, fire up that kerosene lantern I've rigged and heat this water over it."

Mark did as he was told, and within ten minutes, Olms was satisfied he had cleaned and bandaged Clint as well as he could and that God was going to have to do the rest of the work of bringing the town hero back to full consciousness.

For Agnes, the doctor just cleaned her head and thumbed back her eyelids to study her pupils. They were dilated—a sure indication that she had a severe concussion.

"What can you do for her?" Mark asked, noting the grim expression on the doctor's face.

"Pray that she lives without permanent brain damage and that the animal who struck her that hard dies and burns in hell."

"And that's all?"

"I'm not trained to do brain surgery!" Doctor Olms immediately lowered his voice. "I'm sorry, Mark. I had no call to yell at you."

The merchant expelled a deep breath. "I heard about Mr. Butler. I can't believe that Blackstone would do that."

"It was him?"

Mark nodded his head. "The bank clerk saw it. He's so shaken up they've taken him over to the saloon and they're pouring whiskey down him."

"Probably just as well," the doctor said. "A sight like that would unhinge many a good mind."

When the doctor had finished cleaning Agnes's wound and taking her pulse, he turned to Lucinda, who was being supported on a divan by two townswomen. Her eyes were closed and her complexion was very pale.

"You gave the powders to her?"

"Yes," one of the women said. "It calmed her down right fast."

The doctor knelt before Lucinda. He took her pulse, thumbed up her eyelids as he had done to Agnes, then nodded. "She'll sleep for twenty-four hours. It's sometimes the best medicine. When she awakens, we'll be here to give her all the comfort we can."

"What can we say if she asks about her father?" one of the women asked.

Olms stood up and passed one hand shakily across his eyes. "If she asks, that means she still has her right mind and I will be very, very happy. It's if she *doesn't* ask that I worry about."

"Mrs. Moore is real bad hurt, isn't she?"

"Yes," Doctor Olms said. "She's real bad."

"We'll have a special church service for her tonight."

"Good. Pray for the dead as well, and for Mr. Adams. He did kill one of the gang, did he not?"

"Yeah," Mark answered with satisfaction. "Shot him right out of the saddle before he saved Miss Lucinda's life."

They all looked at the unconscious man on the examining table, and the doctor summed up all their thoughts when he said, "He's a brave, brave man. A real asset to our community."

"I'll bet the reward on Blackstone and his gang goes to ten thousand dollars after this," Mark said.

"Whatever it takes to catch those animals," the doctor said. "That's what ought to be paid."

"It'll bring every bounty hunter in the West to Carson City," the feed-store owner predicted. "It'll bring the good and the bad along with them. You mark my words."

The doctor nodded and then went over to examine Agnes again before her husband arrived from their little ranch. Agnes was his friend—she was everyone's friend—and one of the most popular merchants in town.

Doctor Olms shook his head. He felt her feeble, racing pulse. He did not think she was going to live through the rest of the day, and maybe that was a blessing, because he had a feeling that her poor little brains were all scrambled up inside.

Damn Harry Blackstone and his rabid animals! Damn them to an everlasting hell!

"Doctor?"

Olms looked up to see the young bank clerk stagger inside, holding his head. "I was pistol-whipped, too," the young man said, looking dazed and scared.

"Sit down, son. How much of our money did they get?"

"All of it," the clerk said. "Over forty-eight thousand dollars. Your savings, my savings, everybody's savings."

Olms shook his head. Well, he thought, if the money isn't recovered, I guess it just means that I was meant to die practicing medicine.

"Someone will catch them and get back the money," he said aloud, but without being able to generate much confidence in his voice. "Now you just sit down over here while I get some hot water and bandages. And while you're sitting, just thank the Lord that you're still alive."

"I already have," the clerk said in a trembling voice. "I have a bunch of times already. I never seen anyone like them. They laughed when Blackstone slit Mr. Butler's throat. They laughed!"

The young man's voice was rising toward hysteria, so Doctor Olms began to search for some more opium powder.

THREE

Lucinda Butler was trying to control her grief, trying to keep from breaking down completely as the hearse rolled into Carson City's cemetery. Her father, the most prominent of those who had been killed by the Blackstone Gang, was in the town's only hearse, which was followed by a procession of buckboards draped in black crepe paper and carrying the bodies of Agnes and the two brave townsmen who had been gunned down while trying to stop the bank robbery.

Lucinda sniffled and squared her shoulders. Since the death of her father, she'd devoted almost all of her waking hours to the care of the Gunsmith, who even now remained unconscious in bed. Would he ever recover? And if so, would he be permanently brain-damaged? The very possibility of that filled Lucinda with dread.

Overhead, an iron-gray ceiling of clouds blanketed the sky, and up on the Sierra Nevadas, Lucinda could hear the rumble of thunder and could see flashes of lightning skipping over the highest peaks. A cold wind whipped at her face, blowing grit from the grassless cemetery into everyone's eyes.

Behind Lucinda, a heavyset woman in her thirties with two children broke down and began to sob hysterically as the buckboard carrying her husband's body passed. Several of her friends tried to hold her erect, but the heavy woman crumbled at the knees and dropped to the ground, weeping

19

and wailing while her two young children looked on, dumb with confusion and pain.

Doctor Olms stood near the grave of her father. Since the mortician was an indecisive man, the doctor took charge of the unloading of bodies, and within a very few minutes, the caskets were all given to their final resting places.

The minister, a short, blocky man with a thick mane of silver hair, opened the Bible and began to read, but Lucinda did not hear a word he said. She was remembering her father, a good man, a well-loved and generous man in this community, who had died trying to protect their savings.

When the Scripture readings were finished, the minister slowly closed the Bible, then raised his head to survey the huge gathering. It was the largest funeral he had ever conducted, and he was a little nervous.

He licked his lips, wiped his eyes of the grit and irritation of the strengthening wind, and then said, "We all come today to honor our brave dead. They were good men and women who gave their lives trying to protect this community's savings. The fact that they failed has nothing to do with the honor that we shower them with this day."

The minister raised a finger and shook it at the approaching thunderstorms that were now booming over the Sierras. "And this day, I assure you, the Lord will remember who killed these men and—for all eternity—they will burn in everlasting hell while our brave friends and loved ones buried here will bask in eternal salvation and the glory of the Lord."

Lucinda took comfort and was strengthened by this promise. In her heart there burned pain but also a hunger for vengeance against the Blackstone Gang, particularly against their leader, Harry Blackstone, who had slit her father's throat as if he were a goat to be slaughtered.

Thunder rolled, and across the city, moving from west to east and the cemetery, a dark storm cloud raced in on them.

Horses stomped nervously, while men and women stood torn between their desire to honor these brave dead and to protect themselves from what they knew would be a cold rain and a hard, biting wind.

"And so," the minister continued as his hat went sailing off over the gravestones, bouncing and spinning toward the Comstock Lode, "today, we lay to rest our loved ones and pray to the Lord that they will rest in His loving arms forever and ever. Amen."

At the word *amen*, everyone scattered like leaves in a storm, racing for cover and for their horses. The buckboards were turned around and sent flying out of the cemetery. The minister and mortician took cover inside the refuge of the glass-enclosed hearse, while some poor employee had to climb up onto its front seat and drive it back into the center of town.

"Come," the doctor said, taking Lucinda's arm and shielding her from the wind, "get inside my carriage."

The doctor was a reasonably wealthy man in his own right—or at least he had been until most of his savings were stolen by the Blackstone Gang. He had had the foresight and the resources to hire a driver, so they both climbed into his fine carriage and slammed the door, then felt the coach rock on its heavy leather straps as their driver turned the rig around and headed back toward town at a brisk trot.

"So," the doctor said, as the rain began to pelt the roof of their carriage, "we need to talk about your situation a moment. I want to help if I can."

"I am well taken care of," said Lucinda. "Even though my father lost a great deal of money in that robbery, he had extensive investments in commercial and residential properties along with Comstock mining shares that will provide for me very nicely."

The doctor relaxed. "Good!" he said. "I had supposed that

your father would do something like that. He was, you know, my very best friend."

Lucinda patted the doctor on the arm. She had been so absorbed in her own grief and loss that she had selfishly failed to even consider that Doctor Olms would also be deeply grieving.

"And what about you, Doctor? Do you also have assets besides the savings you placed in my father's bank?"

"Fortunately, I do. But only because your father insisted that I diversify my investments. I would have put it all in his trust, but he made sure that I spread my money around a little so that I would be protected no matter what the calamity. I have stock in the Virginia City mines that alone will carry me quite comfortably to the grave, even if I never recover a dime from the savings that were absconded from the bank. Unfortunately, I am quite unique in this respect. Many of those at the cemetery that you saw today lost everything to the Blackstone Gang."

"Then we must help them," Lucinda said. "I will set up a fund and use all my money to make sure that everyone who had savings at my father's bank will be repaid."

"That is very generous," the doctor said, "and I'll help. Let's just hope that someone recovers the money and spares all of us the heartaches. Both of us are comfortably fixed but not nearly enough that we can compensate the huge loss of that robbery."

"I know," Lucinda said, "but right now, all I can think about is Clint Adams and how he might never recover. He . . . he took the bullets that should have been mine!"

Lucinda broke down, and the doctor folded her in his arms as the storm crashed and boomed all around them and the cottonwood trees along the main street groaned and bent to the wind.

"Do you want to know something?" the doctor asked.

"What?" Lucinda sniffled.

"I believe that Clint Adams is going to make a complete recovery and that it will happen any day now."

She wiped her eyes and smiled through her tears. "Really?"

"Yes. I have seen signs of recovery. His reflexes, for example. I have been testing them all along to determine the amount, if any, of brain damage or malfunctioning. Yesterday, I found none at all."

Lucinda hugged the old doctor's neck. "I think I love him," she said. "He's my hero, as you are."

Doctor Olms smiled proudly and listened to the rainstorm outside, glad that he was dry and holding a girl that he loved as if he were her own father—which he was, now that her real father had been laid to rest.

"Is it true that the Blackstone Gang attacked and robbed the V. and T. Railroad?" Lucinda asked just before they arrived at the livery.

"That's what I heard," Olms said. "They jumped it on the grade when it was barely moving and quickly shot the fireman and made the engineer stop the train. Within ten minutes they had blasted open the bank car and shot to death the two unfortunate guards hired to protect the money. Others robbed the passengers. A young woman was taken as hostage."

"Oh, dear heavens!" Lucinda cried. "Anyone we might have heard of?"

"I don't think so," the doctor said gravely. "She was a half-breed girl, from what I've heard. Her mother was a Paiute squaw and her father was a prospector. I guess the young woman was about your age."

"Lord have mercy on her!" Lucinda exclaimed as she tried not to imagine what would have happened to herself if she had fallen into the hands of Harry Blackstone and his gang of depraved animals.

"Yes," the doctor said, wishing he had not even brought the subject up. "They formed a posse up on the Comstock, but you know those miners. They seem interested in little except drinking, playing games of chance, and . . . well, never mind. Suffice to say, they were a sorry collection—most not even qualified to ride a horse. They returned after a day of hunting and had no success."

Lucinda's fists clenched. "*Someone* has to stop them!"

"They will," the doctor said, trying to hold his own anger and frustration in check. "It's just that the army is so busy trying to protect the settlers and miners from the Paiutes, who are threatening to go on the warpath again. And as for the regular United States marshal and the sheriff of Virginia City, they are completely overtaxed trying to solve the almost daily occurrence of murder and mayhem that takes place up there. So it's going to be up to the bounty hunters, unless I miss my guess."

"What is the reward now?"

"Ten thousand for Harry Blackstone, alive or dead. Two thousand each for his gang members, most all of whom have been identified and placed on wanted posters."

"If I were a man I'd get a gun and go hunting them myself!" Lucinda swore.

The doctor felt the carriage roll to a stop beside the livery. "Of course you would," he said. "But I think that there will be plenty of men out hunting for that gang now that the bounty has been raised so high. Why, they didn't offer that much for Billy the Kid! Don't you worry—the end is near for Harry Blackstone and his killers."

Lucinda nodded and was helped down from the carriage. "I had better go over to see Clint now. I didn't want to leave his side, but Mrs. Hanson promised to watch him closely."

"She's a competent nurse," the doctor said. "Besides, you would never have forgiven yourself for not attending your father's funeral."

"I know, but I worry that Blackstone might seek vengeance against Clint. After all, the Gunsmith did kill one of his men."

"Blackstone is a monster and he is very intelligent," the

doctor said. "The man isn't going to risk his life trying to gain a little revenge."

"But I thought he once said that if anyone killed one of his men, he would personally make sure they died."

"The source of that quote was not reliable. And even if it were accurate, it would just prove how intelligent Blackstone really is, because the threat is designed to drive fear into the hearts of his victims."

"I know, but . . ."

The doctor smiled to comfort her. "Please don't concern yourself about that hollow threat. Clint Adams is safe at your house. I'm sure of it, and so is our sheriff. If we weren't, he would be guarded day and night."

"Yes," Lucinda said, "I'm sure you're right."

Lucinda hurried away in the rain, calling back to the doctor that she would expect him for his usual afternoon tea.

FOUR

The thunder sounded like cannon fire, and the lightning that shivered across the heavens lit up the stormy sky, transforming the Gunsmith's room to a brilliant, shimmering white.

His eyes fluttered open, and the next cannon shot brought him bolt upright in his bed.

"It's all right, Mr. Adams," the old woman said, getting up and padding softly over to the curtains, which she opened to watch the storm. "It's just a storm passing over the mountains and we'll be fine. Lordy, is it good to see you awaken!"

The woman returned to Clint's bedside, where he sat blinking with confusion. "You've been unconscious for almost three days now. But none of us ever lost hope that you'd be fine. Not for a minute."

Clint reached up and felt the heavy bandage wrapped turban-like around his head. "Where am I?"

"In Miss Lucinda Butler's house. In her bedroom, in fact. She's been sleeping in the parlor and I've been helping spell her. The poor girl has been at your side most day and night."

Clint took a deep, steadying breath. He could remember nothing since taking the bullet to the skull. "Where . . . where is she now?"

Mrs. Hanson's brow furrowed. "Miss Lucinda is at her father's funeral, Mr. Adams. It's a sad, sad day for this town. We lost four good men to that holdup. Yours was the only gun

27

that brought one of them down."

"Who else was killed in the holdup?"

"Besides Mr. Butler, there was two other men and Agnes Moore."

Clint's hands clenched at his sides. "Agnes died! But why?"

"She must have tried to fight them," Mrs. Hanson said. "She was in the bank when the gang went to hold it up and she must have done something, because the doctor said someone pistol-whipped her so bad she never woke up. Died just yesterday, she did. Had a special service for her last evening at the Methodist church. Lots and lots of people come. Agnes was well loved and admired, same as Mr. Butler."

Clint swung his feet out from under the covers, causing Mrs. Hanson to exclaim, "Oh, Mr. Adams, you can't get up just yet! You won't have any strength after four days in bed."

"Get my pants," he said. "And where's my gun?"

"But—"

"Just do as I ask, Mrs. Hanson! Please don't argue with me!"

The poor woman was upset, and she looked ready to start crying as she brought Clint his gun and pants. Feeling guilty, Clint lowered his voice. "Listen, I apologize but—"

They both heard the back door open and footsteps coming up the hall.

"Miss Lucinda," the woman called as she stepped out into the hallway, "you better get in here and try to talk some sense into this man. He won't stay in bed and—"

Clint heard the woman scream, and then he heard the very familiar sound of a gun striking a soft skull and then the sound of the woman hitting the floor. The Gunsmith's instincts were slowed by his injury, but they were good enough to warn him that something terrible was happening and that it sure as hell was not Lucinda Butler in the hallway.

Clint snatched his gun from its holster and rolled sideways to topple off the side of the bed. The bed was wedged close to the wall and he could not extricate himself all that well, but when two men jumped into the doorway and opened fire, their bullets plowed through the heavy mattress and whanged off the bedsprings.

Clint's body dropped to the floor behind the bed. Rather than try to fight his way back up to mattress level, he flattened and let the men bang away. He could feel the slugs eating into the wall and he knew that Lucinda's room was being destroyed, but he held his fire until the shooting stopped and then poked his gun under the bed, tried to guess where the doorway was, and started squeezing his own trigger.

Clint fired four blind shots under the bed, hoping that he could wound his attackers—maybe blow their ankles or knees apart with a little luck. And when he stopped firing he knew he had gotten lucky, because he could hear a man screaming and cursing in agony.

Clint cursed a blue streak himself as he tried to squeeze his way back up the wall so that he could finish off whoever had come to assassinate him. Maybe if he were real lucky, it would be Harry Blackstone himself, come to carry out his threat of retaliation.

But by the time Clint was able to force his arms and torso over the mattress and line his gun sight on the doorway, there was no one to shoot. He saw plenty of blood on the floor, however, and he could hear grunting in the hallway; it did not take a great deal of imagination to figure that it was the man he'd wounded, now trying to escape.

Clint hauled himself out from behind the bed, rolled across the mattress, and jumped toward the door. What he had failed to account for, however, was that his legs would betray him because of their inactivity during his recovery.

His legs buckled and Clint toppled forward, struck the floor, and rolled into the hallway just as he saw the silhouettes of two men. One was down and being dragged toward the back door, but the instant Clint appeared, the other man who'd been helping him suddenly swung a double-barreled shotgun up to waist level and pulled both triggers.

The blast was incredible in the close confines of the hall. Clint actually felt a deadly wind pass overhead, and then the hallway was filled with smoke. He managed to get his gun up and he emptied it, taking care to bracket his shots so that his chances of hitting the upright gunman were optimized.

The door slammed. Clint crawled to his feet, staggered forward, and pitched over Mrs. Hanson and crashed forward. He got back up but tripped again over a body before he could beat his way through the heavy gunsmoke and reach the outdoors.

He was a sight as he staggered out into Miss Lucinda's backyard, clad only in his long johns. But the worst part was that when he saw Harry Blackstone astride a tall board fence, Clint's gun was empty.

Blackstone's wasn't. The outlaw leader dropped his empty shotgun and reached for his six-shooter. Their eyes locked, and then the Gunsmith threw himself sideways behind a stone wall.

Blackstone's bullets whined meanly off the rocks, and Clint heard the vicious outlaw leader scream, "I'll get you, Adams! No one kills my men and lives!"

Clint hugged the flower garden and prayed that Blackstone did not get it in his mind to come off the top of the fence and get him that very moment. If he did Clint knew he was as good as dead. His gun was empty; he had no cartridge belt strapped around his waist and therefore no extra bullets.

Up the street a dog was barking furiously, and Clint could hear shouts. Blackstone cursed again and then dropped off the fence and disappeared up the alley. Clint knew from the shape his rubbery legs were in that it would be a futile gesture to attempt to cross Lucinda's backyard and scale her board fence.

So instead of going after Blackstone, he pushed himself erect and staggered back into the hallway.

An outlaw lay soiling Lucinda's carpet with his blood. Clint grabbed the man by his boots and dragged him out on the back porch, and the effort took all of his remaining strength. Next Clint staggered down the hallway and found Mrs. Hanson. She was already coming awake, and the Gunsmith heaved a great sigh of relief.

He went back to the dying outlaw and took a good look at his gray face. "What's your name?"

The man's eyelids fluttered open and he stared at Clint for several seconds before he began to throw his eyes around at the house, the tree limbs, and the sky above. Clint had been forced to kill a lot of men over the years, and he knew that this one was quickly fading.

"What's your name?" he repeated, kneeling beside the dying assassin. "If you have a mother or someone you want me to let know you died, then I'll get word to them."

The man's face twisted with hatred and his lips moved as he struggled to speak. Thinking that he wanted to give him a relative's name, Clint leaned closer, and that's when the killer tried to spit in his face.

Rage filled the Gunsmith, and he momentarily lost control. He grabbed the dying man by the shirtfront and shook him. "You murdering bastard!" he shouted into the man's gray face. "I hope you rot in hell!"

"Fuck you," the outlaw choked in a strangled whisper the very moment before he died.

Clint slammed the body down against the porch floor and climbed unsteadily to his feet. He threw open the back door and wobbled down the hallway to help the dazed woman who lay groaning on the carpet.

"Clint!"

He cradled Mrs. Hanson's head in his lap.

"Clint!"

Lucinda came racing down the hallway to hug him, and then she almost fainted when she saw Mrs. Hanson's bleeding head.

"She's going to have a headache," Clint said with reassurance, "but otherwise she'll be fine."

Lucinda kissed Clint's mouth and began to cry. "You're . . . you're all right!"

"Yeah," he said, holding the girl tight, "but just as soon as I get strong again, I'm going after Harry Blackstone and his gang. I'm going to either bring them in or kill them off one by one. And when I do I'll get your money back, or else I'll turn the reward back to the people who need it the most."

"I want to help you," she sniffled into his neck.

"No," Clint said in a hard-edged voice. "This used to be my line of work, and I do it best alone."

Lucinda hugged him tighter, and then the doctor and a whole lot of other people who'd been alerted by the sound of gunfire came crowding into the hallway. Clint wished he'd had time to pull on his pants before all the action began.

FIVE

In the rock basement of his Gold Hill Hotel, Harry Blackstone studied his reflection in a mirror and told himself to relax: There would be another time when he could kill the Gunsmith and do it slowly.

"Timing," he reminded himself out loud, "is everything in life."

And how well he understood that! Once he had been a promising New York actor, an extraordinarily handsome young man with a future as bright as the shimmering stars. But then he had been cursed with love and had the extreme bad timing and misfortune to walk in on his fiancée while she was in the embrace of a senator's rich young son. In a fit of jealous rage, Blackstone had bludgeoned them both to death with his silver-headed walking cane. And then, in a crazed fit, he had taken a small pen knife and slashed both his love and her lover.

Within the hour he had fled New York. Because of the senator's prominence, he was relentlessly pursued even to the Barbary Coast, where he had again succumbed to the lure of fame and tried to make a stage comeback. But luck had betrayed him once more and he had been driven from San Francisco and into hiding by Pinkerton agents hired by the vengeful senator.

Still on the run and having become a master of disguise, Blackstone had arrived in Virginia City, drawn by the faint hope of returning to the boards at Piper's Opera House, where such great thespians, singers, and entertainers as Lily Langtry, John Drew, Lotta Crabtree, and Edwin Booth had performed. And while it was true that the Comstock miners preferred bawdy comedies and cock- or dogfights to great theater, Blackstone was confident he could elevate the fare being offered at Piper's if only he had the funds to buy and refurbish the stately old building.

But the price was high. Not that the old building itself was so valuable, because it was not. In some other town—any other town except the one that rested on the richest vein of gold and silver in the world—Blackstone could have had the building for a few thousand dollars. But in Virginia City, the asking price was one hundred thousand, take it or leave it, because that was the value of the property if the building were razed and sold as a mining claim.

Until Blackstone had seized upon the idea of using his theatrical training and skills to disguise himself and become an outlaw, such a huge sum of money would have made the acquisition impossible. But now, with luck and timing and another ten or so holdups, he would be able to make his dream come true.

Timing and luck. On the stage, even while performing vaudeville, his timing was impeccable. But in love, Blackstone thought of himself as the most unlucky wretch imaginable. But now, by playing his part as Nevada's most wanted killer and outlaw, he was fast becoming a very wealthy man. In six more months he would be rich, and not only would he buy Piper's Opera House, but he would turn it into a glittering palace of culture and refinement. He would allow no more sleazy entertainment, and every patron who came would be required to wear a shirt and shoes before checking his six-gun and his bottle of hard liquor at the door.

Yes, Blackstone thought as he prepared to remove his

disguise, all it takes is good timing, luck, guts, and a lot of money. With a wave of his hand, Blackstone bid his outlaw self farewell and peeled off a fake black mustache, eyebrows, spade beard, and wig to reveal a rather handsome and light-complexioned man with blond hair and eyebrows. He was, by necessity, clean-shaven.

Blackstone changed his shirt, his lip curling because of the spotted blood. Damn the Gunsmith! he raged silently. I almost had the man.

A knock on his door brought him around, and he hurriedly shoved his disguise into a cloth bag, which he carefully hid behind a loose rock in the basement wall.

"Who is it?" he said, looking at himself again in the mirror before he smoothed his hair.

"It's Deke."

Deke was Blackstone's only confidant, the one man who knew his real identity. Deke was his right arm, the enforcer who recruited members of the Blackstone Gang and "discharged" them into eternal rest when they disobeyed a command or in some way disappointed their leader.

"Come on in," Blackstone said, turning to face his lieutenant.

Deke had no last name nor did he admit to a past. Blackstone had found the man in Carson City's state prison and managed to bribe a parole for the inmate in return for certain promises.

"What is it?" Blackstone asked in a clipped voice.

"It's that half-breed girl we took off the train. She's raisin' hell again upstairs. I think you'd better talk to her, sir. Maybe give her some more medicine."

"Yes," Blackstone said, "perhaps I shall."

Deke was a thick slab of a man, only about five-foot-eight but weighing well over two hundred pounds. He was all gristle, bone, and muscle, and Blackstone had chosen him because he was a remorseless killer, an expert with a gun or a bowie knife.

"I could make her shut up," Deke offered hopefully. "Give me ten minutes and I'd make her shut up."

"I'm sure you would," Blackstone said, "but I have my own ideas about how to handle women."

Deke's round face broke into a smile that revealed he was missing several of his front teeth. "Yeah, sure you do," he chortled. "And I'll bet your way is a hell of a lot more fun!"

Blackstone was repulsed by the man, and yet he knew that Deke suited his purposes quite nicely. He was loyal, brave, and stupid enough to control but wise enough to know when to keep his mouth shut.

"Go on up and tell her I'll be along in a few minutes with relief," Blackstone said.

Deke nodded and left as Blackstone found a clothes brush and cleaned his suit, then polished his boots. He noted a tear in his trousers from where he had scaled the fence. This angered him, and he again thought of the Gunsmith and how he would one day kill the famous exlawman.

Blackstone selected a frock coat from a closet in his basement, and then he doused himself with cologne before he went to see the captive half-breed girl.

Her name was Veronica and she was extraordinarily beautiful, which was, of course, the reason he had not been able to resist taking her hostage. Blackstone was still in his thirties, and a man in good health had his physical needs to satisfy. Whores disgusted him, and although as one of Virginia City's most eligible bachelors and the owner of a hotel, he could have taken his pick of many pretty young women, marriage was far too risky. Sooner or later an intelligent bride would realize that her actor-husband led two very different lives, and then she might have to be eliminated.

Far better, Blackstone thought, to simply have a beautiful concubine, even one who was an unwilling wildcat. The half-breed girl represented a great challenge, but Blackstone was quite sure that he could tame and gentle her ferocious spirit. He had blindfolded her before bringing her to his hotel, so she had no idea where she might be; and there was little chance that she could escape, because Deke was watching her constantly and enjoying every minute of it—until she started cursing and spitting at him like a little animal.

Blackstone hurried upstairs to the room in which Veronica was being held. When he opened her door, he saw that Deke had tied her hands and feet to the bed and stuffed a dirty stocking in her mouth to keep her quiet.

"She'll tear out your eyes, boss. You'd better be careful."

"I will," said Blackstone, with more assurance than he felt. "Now go outside and leave us alone."

"You gonna do it to her?" Deke blurted, his little deep-set eyes radiating his own desire. "I'd like to watch if you are."

"Get out!" Blackstone said in a hard voice.

Deke got out, and then Blackstone pulled a chair up beside the girl. "I suppose I could take that filthy stocking out of your mouth but then you'd scream, wouldn't you?"

The girl stopped struggling and glared at him with hate-filled eyes.

"Of course you would," Blackstone said. "Well then, I'll just have to leave the gag in your mouth until you decide to cooperate."

Blackstone touched her dress. "This is a rag, do you know that? I could dress you in silk and sequins. Can you sing as prettily as you look? If so, I could make you a great attraction at Piper's Opera House. Do know that you are beautiful? Your face reminds me so strongly of the famed Lola Montez that when I first saw you on that train it took my breath away, and I thought you were her—only in her youth, when she was the most beautiful woman in Europe."

The girl had stopped struggling, and the hatred in her eyes had been replaced by curiosity. As an actor, Blackstone had developed a rich, deep voice that was nothing short of mesmerizing.

"Let me tell you something," Blackstone said. "Once upon a time there was a beautiful girl who lived in filth and squalor. She met a poor boy and they fell in love, had children, and lived all their lives very poor. And before too long, the beautiful girl's face became old and harsh because she was always hungry and bitter."

Blackstone smiled. "Do you like that story, Veronica?"

Veronica shook her head.

"All right then, how about this story: Once upon a time there was a beautiful young girl who did not fall in love but met a very rich man who wanted to help her. Of course, he insisted they sleep together, but for this he would be very, very generous. He would teach the girl how to be a lady, one well mannered, and then he would teach her how to sing, act, and dance. And she became loved and very famous because of this man, and because of it she fell in love with him and they traveled the world together in triumph, giving performances everywhere to huge, adoring audiences. And they were very happy."

Blackstone smiled again. "Did you like the second story better?"

Veronica nodded her head.

"Good," Blackstone said, "because it can be *our* story. It is up to you. I will, if you want, take you out in the desert and you might find your way back to the Comstock. On the other hand, you might fall into the hands of the Paiutes or some mining men out there who would not treat you kindly. I think you can guess what they would do to you out in the desert. Can't you?"

Veronica nodded again, more vigorously this time.

Blackstone pulled the gag from her mouth, and his forefinger brushed her lips, then trailed down to the prominent mound of one breast. "I can make you rich and famous, Veronica, and ask but little in return. It is your choice. Tell me what you choose: the desert or dreams of fame you cannot even begin to imagine all coming true."

Veronica looked up at his face. It was a nice face, though his eyes scared her and looked a little crazy. But he talked so well. He was obviously an educated man—maybe even a rich man. Her own circumstances were very bad. She had no mother or father. The wealthy man who had taken her to work at his big house in Virginia City had raped her, and she had been running away from him when this one had robbed the train and taken her hostage. Could her life become any worse even if he were a little crazy and only half of his promises came true?

Veronica did not think so.

"I can sing," she whispered. "I will sing something for you."

He leaned forward and kissed her forehead, then her eyelids, and then her neck. "Sing," he whispered.

Veronica found that her heart was banging against her chest, and she could scarcely breathe as he unbuttoned her cheap, flimsy blouse. When his lips found her breast, she took a sharp intake of breath, and in a clear and pure voice she began a song she had learned called "Love Is a Flower in Spring."

Blackstone sat up and listened as he untied and undressed her. His heart was pounding too, but as much with joy as with desire, because, indeed, Veronica had the voice of a dark angel. Her voice was strong and untutored, but Blackstone knew that he could train it well, just as he could train the lovely creature to dance and become a great stage presence. One worthy to be his partner in his Piper's Opera House as well as in the gilded palaces of London, Paris, and Rome.

When his lips traced lightly down her flat stomach and touched her thighs, Veronica's voice broke. Her fingers intertwined into his thick mane of blond hair and she pushed him lower and lower, until his tongue entered her body and she stiffened with sweet pleasure.

"Please," she begged, "I want to do what you ask and be famous. I want to dream and be poor no more. Help me!"

Blackstone raised his head and chuckled softly; then his tongue slipped back into her womanhood again and he gripped her hard buttocks. It was strange, he thought: He had been unlucky in love, but whenever he wanted a woman's body without her heart, he had it for the taking. And what a woman this one was!

Blackstone's skilled tongue probed and laved, caressed and pleasured, until the woman was moaning and her thighs were gripping his head and her buttocks were pumping like pistons.

He stopped and left her trembling with unfulfilled desire.

"Oh, please," she begged as he began to undress, "hurry!"

Blackstone took his time. He knew that her desire would ebb until he mounted her, but then he would bring it back stronger than before.

She opened herself to him, moaning as his manhood began to plunge in and out of her surging body.

"Sing now," he ordered.

Her eyes opened wide and he was staring into them. She swallowed with fear and pleasure, then did as he told her and began to sing as he worked over her, coaxing her body to yield itself completely.

Veronica closed her eyes and sang until she felt herself exploding with desire and she could not speak, so great was her pleasure. She gripped him to her and he took her breath away as his body spilled its hot seed and he roared like a lion in her ear.

Veronica lost her mind for a few moments, and when she went limp, he again stiffened on her and then he too relaxed.

"You have not had many men, have you?" he asked.

In truth, she had had more than ten but never one like this. All the others had been boys or brutes who had used her simply as a receptacle, battering her body until their own needs were met. But this man, crazy or sane, had done things to her that she had not believed possible.

"Who are you?" she panted.

"I am your mentor and your master," Blackstone said. "I am everything to you now."

Veronica hugged him tightly. And she believed.

SIX

Lucinda brought a tray of sandwiches into the bedroom and placed it at Clint's side. "How are you feeling this evening?"

"I'm feeling fine," he said. "In fact, I'm beginning to feel downright slothful. I think I'm ready to get back on my feet and—"

Lucinda placed her cool fingers across Clint's lips. "Shhh," she whispered, "you know that you're not in any physical condition yet to be up and about."

Clint removed her hand and pulled her close, not giving a damn if he squashed the sandwiches. He kissed her mouth, and when she sighed, he slipped his hand up her dress and began caressing her shapely thigh.

"Clint Adams!" she cried, struggling out of his grasp. "Whatever is the matter with you!"

"Not a damn thing," he said, miffed at her reaction, "that a little passionate lovin' wouldn't cure."

Lucinda blushed. "Mr. Adams, really!"

"Yeah, really," he said, realizing that he wasn't getting anywhere. "The only way I'm going to stay in this bed is if you join me in it."

Lucinda's big blue eyes widened with shock and she rocked back to her feet. "Honestly, Mr. Adams! I can't have you speaking to me that way."

"Suit yourself," Clint said, throwing the covers aside and

climbing to his feet as he reached for his pants and Lucinda averted her eyes. "But the fact of the matter is that I mean to find that Harry Blackstone and put a hangman's noose around his neck before he kills any more folks—including myself."

Clint got his pants on, and he grunted with pain as he tried to get his shirt over his left shoulder. Lucinda heard him and she turned. "Here," she said, "let me help you."

Clint let her help. She wouldn't meet his eyes but she stood very close, and he swore he could hear her heart beating like a trip-hammer.

"What are you afraid of?" he asked her quietly. "I wouldn't hurt you. I'd make you feel . . . wonderful."

She looked up at him. "I'm afraid of it," she whispered.

"It wouldn't hurt," he assured her, "not if a man knows what he's doing."

"I wasn't speaking of a physical pain, though I suppose there is that to endure. What I meant was an emotional pain."

"I don't follow."

Lucinda swallowed dryly. "I . . . I just know too many women whose hearts have been broken after they've given the man they love their . . . their . . . "

"Bodies," he said, seeing how acutely embarrassed she was by this subject and the intimacy of the conversation. "Help me pull on my boots, will you?"

She seemed eager to do something rather than pursue the conversation. She grabbed his boots, dropped to her hands and knees, and strained to help him pull them on.

"Thanks," he said, when they were finally on tight. He reached down and helped her back to her feet. "Lucinda, I wish I could tell you what it could be like for us. But I can't, because I'm not that good with words. I can only say that it would be better than anything you can imagine. It would be . . . it would be glorious, my dear."

She forced a smile. "I'm sure that it would with the man

I love. And you are that man, Clint. But you're so wild and unpredictable. You've told me you want to settle down and build up your gunsmithing business, but what I'm hearing now is that you really intend to go on a manhunt."

"What choice do I have?" he asked. "Harry Blackstone came into this very house to kill me. I have no evidence that says he won't try it again. And what about poor Agnes? And your father? And the two other men who died trying to prevent the robbery?"

Lucinda blinked back tears. "I know about them! I think about them all the time, and I want justice, too! But not if it means that you'll be killed as well as other men who try to capture that vicious gang!"

Clint reached out and put his hands on her shoulders. "Dear Lucinda, you are so very, very naive. Do you really think any of this will stop or go away? Do you think that the gang will just disappear or decide that they've robbed enough people and retire?"

"Maybe they will."

"No," he said patiently, "it is a fact of nature that things always want to grow or grab more of whatever they have and like. Among peaceful, law-abiding men, it is called ambition. Among outlaws, well, it's greed, and it leads to murder unless it is checked. Blackstone is like a lone wolf that has killed a sheep and found it easy and tasty. He's developed confidence and a taste for blood and money. Nothing will stop a man like that except a man like me. Do you understand?"

Lucinda shook her head. "I hate violence. And the taking of a human life breaks one of the Ten Commandments. And yet I'm sure that you're right about Mr. Blackstone and his gang. And only a depraved animal would slice . . . "

Lucinda could not go on, and she burst out in tears. Clint held her close and let her cry it out. "You're just too gentle a woman for a man like me and the frontier life. Maybe the best thing for you to do would be to take your money and go back East where things are more refined. Where an independently wealthy young lady doesn't have to see the hard side of life."

She sniffled. "I couldn't do that. I feel like I owe the depositors of my father's bank. And I will repay them all, even if it leaves me penniless. I've made up my mind about that. They trusted my father and his bank, and that trust will be vindicated."

Clint knew that Lucinda wasn't just talking an empty promise. The young woman meant what she said, and it bothered him a great deal to think that she might wind up without any funds of her own.

"You just hang onto your money," he said, "because I'm going to catch Blackstone and recover the cash. And even if I don't, someone else will sooner or later. The man isn't a ghost. He has to have a hiding place, and someone must see him use it."

"Do you even have any idea where to start looking for him?"

Clint had to shake his head. "I'm afraid not. But I've done this kind of work too many years to believe that an entire gang can just be swallowed up as if by magic. They're hiding somewhere within a hundred miles of here, I'll guarantee that much."

"A hundred miles?" Lucinda smiled with tolerance. "A hundred miles to the west you are almost in California's great central valley. A hundred miles south you are nearing Death Valley and . . ."

It was Clint's turn to place his fingers on her lips. "Listen," he said, "I didn't tell you that I thought tracking this gang down was going to be easy. I'm sure that, because of the huge reward being offered for them, there are a lot of bounty hunters out there right now who are looking for Blackstone and his gang. All I'm saying is that I believe I can do better because I *have* to do better. For you and for myself. I mean to get that man before he gets me, and I mean to see you keep your inheritance."

She handed him his black Stetson. "When he learns that you've gotten out of bed and taken up Blackstone's trail, Doctor Olms is going to have a fit, you know."

"Yeah," Clint said, "I'm sure he will. But I'll pay him a visit and explain. Besides, maybe Blackstone's trail starts here. It's as good a place as any to begin looking for some clues."

"Will you come back tonight?"

Clint reached out and kissed her again. "I don't think you're ready for me yet, Miss Butler. But you think about it for a while."

"You're my hero," she told him. "You risked your life to save mine."

"That's because you're so damn much prettier and wealthier than I am," he said, with a wink that make her smile.

Clint strapped on his gun and left Lucinda on her porch. He sure would have liked to stay in bed—with her. But business before pleasure, as his old man always used to say.

SEVEN

When the Gunsmith had been a sheriff, the thing that had most irked him was not knowing when someone was gunning for someone else in the area of his jurisdiction. If a bounty hunter had reason to believe that an outlaw was hiding in Clint's town, then Clint wanted to know about it before the bullets started to fly and maybe someone innocent like himself got shot by mistake.

So as soon as Clint left Lucinda Butler's fine home, he marched down the street and his first stop was the sheriff's office. He knew Sheriff Ben Williamson but not very well, and he figured it was time they got much better acquainted.

Williamson was a large, florid-faced man with an aquiline nose, too much fat around his belt, and a full salt-and-pepper beard that said he was on the shady side of forty. Clint had not yet formed an impression of the man except to suspect that he was better at winning elections and buffaloing drunken miners and cowboys than he was at apprehending hard-nosed killers and outlaws.

"Well, well!" Williamson said as he kicked his big boots off his scarred desk and dropped them heavily to a plank floor that had never seen a broom. "Lookee what we have here! Good to see you up and about, man! I thought you'd probably play it smart and stay at Miss Butler's place at least until Christmas!"

It was meant to be a joke, but Clint didn't think it very funny, and he didn't like the way that the sheriff winked as if they were in on some lewd little secret together about Miss Butler.

"What can you tell me about the robbery?" Clint asked in a blunt tone of voice.

Williamson's grin dissolved into a frown. "Well listen here now, Mr. Adams. I know that you are a pretty famous *hombre* and all that. But in my town you're just another merchant, and this here investigation is confidential law business."

Clint formed his opinion right there and then of the man: Williamson was a lot of hot air and hog fat. "It's also *my* business," he snapped. "Blackstone and his men twice tried to kill me—once during the bank robbery and then again just a few days ago. It's clear enough that he means to exact a revenge against me."

"Maybe, but you've killed two of his men, so maybe he's smart enough to let you be from now on. Anyway, like I said, it's law business."

Clint placed his hands on the desk and leaned over the sheriff. "I'm making it my business, Williamson! So get off your ass and out from behind that shiny badge and start answering my questions!"

The sheriff's face flushed with blood, and, for a minute Clint thought the man was going to fight. Just to make sure that he did not, the Gunsmith put a hand on his gun butt and made it clear that he was in no condition or mood for a brawl.

The sheriff had watery brown eyes, and when they dropped to Clint's gun hand, he gulped and said, "Now just a minute here. No sense in us going after one another."

"That's right. So what can you tell me?"

Williamson had begun to sweat, and he wiped his brow with the back of his sleeve. "Well, sir," he hedged, "I actually ain't been able to find out much. Like everywhere else he's robbed, Blackstone is mighty good at hiding his trail. We formed a posse and lit out after him, but he was long gone. Disappeared in the cottonwoods that run all along the Carson River. We followed the river ten, maybe even fifteen miles, but there were so many tracks we lost those we thought we was followin'. Even an Apache couldn't have kept the tracks straight."

"So," Clint said in a steel-edged voice, "what you're telling me is that you don't know a damn thing and you're sitting here on your fat ass doing nothing about it!"

"Now just a goddamn minute there, mister! I don't have to take that kind of talk from anybody! Not you, not even Wild Bill Hickock himself if he stumbled in here today."

Clint could feel his blood reaching the boiling point. "Did you at least try and find out the names of the gang members I shot?"

"Well of course we did!"

"And?"

Williamson licked his lips nervously. "They been seen by and remembered by a few."

"Where?"

"Around."

Clint clenched his fist and slammed it down on the sheriff's desk so hard that cold coffee jumped from the lawman's filthy cup. "Where exactly!"

"On the Comstock Lode! In Reno. Even here in Carson City and over in Dayton and Genoa. Now, does that help you one damn bit?"

"Yes it does," Clint said. "It helps plenty."

"How?"

Clint wasn't going to answer the sheriff, but a deep voice behind him answered the question anyway. "It tells us that the sonsabitches live hereabouts."

Clint swung around to face the door that he'd left open.

The Gunsmith's eyes dilated and his hand slapped his gun and brought it up in one smooth motion, and he leveled it on the giant's chest.

"It'd be murder," the giant said. "Sheriff, you'd be the witness, and it'd be murder. He'd have to hang any way you'd cut it."

"Big Joe Gritts," Clint hissed. "How'd you get out of prison?"

"I got paroled."

"You should have swung from a rope."

"No rope strong enough to swing me."

"That's where you're wrong."

Gritts smiled through tobacco-stained horse teeth. "You and me," he said, "we can go to the dance later. Right now, the reward for Blackstone and his boys interests me the most."

"You're a bounty hunter?"

"I always figured that it was better to hunt than to be hunted. Especially when the money is so good."

Clint lowered his gun and holstered it. Of all the men he'd tracked down and finally brought to justice, Big Joe Gritts was the meanest, the most dangerous and evil. And the most deserving to hang.

"I've got a score to settle myself with Harry Blackstone," Clint said. "So you'd best keep a long, long way out of my sight."

"It's a free country, and this ain't your town like it was down in Texas. You ain't spit here, Adams. And if you try and stop me again, I'll squash you like a damn dirty bug."

Clint almost went for the man, but that was exactly what Gritts wanted. The giant would have beaten him senseless and enjoyed every minute of it. So instead of falling into Gritt's trap, Clint pushed past the man and headed down the street.

He could hear Gritts's coarse, bawling laughter following him. He'd heard it in Texas and he'd heard it when the man had been sentenced to prison ten years earlier. And once a man heard Big Joe Gritts laugh, he never forgot the sound of it and how it made the hair on the back of his neck stand on end.

EIGHT

The Gunsmith took a long walk to cool down, and then he went into the Washoe Bar and ordered a beer. The arrival of Big Joe Gritts was the last thing in the world he needed at a time like this.

"Afternoon, Clint," the bartender and proprietor said. "Good to see you up and about."

"Thank you, Slim. It's good to be out of bed and on my feet."

A blocky man with the red nose of a drinker chuckled and said, "If'n I was in Miss Lucinda Butler's bed, I'd never get out!"

Clint had just taken hold of his beer, but he didn't have it long. With a sweep of his hand he brought the glass straight into the man's face so perfectly that it centered on his nose and cut a deep circle all the way around it. The man staggered, choking, and Clint filled his dirty mouth with his knuckles and sent him skidding across the barroom floor.

"Anybody else to care to make a comment about Miss Butler?" he asked, in a low but very dangerous tone of voice.

There were about fifteen men drinking in the saloon and not one of them had a word to say, so Clint walked over to the man on the floor, helped him get to his feet, and then grabbed him by the britches and propelled him straight out the door and into the street.

"Give me another beer, and if you don't want to lose a patron for good, then you make sure he isn't here when I am."

"I'll do that, Clint," Slim said, rushing to get another glass and fill it with cool brew.

Men stayed wide apart from the Gunsmith as he drank his beer, ordered another, and then slowly drank it as his mind wrestled with the problem of how he was going to get a lead on Harry Blackstone and his gang.

At last he turned and, with a wave of his hand, disappeared through the door.

"Whew," said Slim, "when it comes to Miss Butler, old Clint, he's as tetchy as a teased snake!"

"Sure is," a man said. "Must mean he thinks mighty highly of her."

"Who wouldn't?" said another. "She's rich, young, and beautiful. Me, I'd crawl naked over hot coals to climb into her bed."

"Any of us would," Slim said, "but we'd sure best not forget to keep it to ourselves when Clint is around."

Everybody nodded and then they went back to drinking, smoking, and playing a little faro and poker.

Clint went directly to the mortician. He did not have much use for the man, but sometimes a mortician saw things that nobody else did and they also got to be pretty good at noticing what was in a dead man's pockets and making sure that it got into their own pockets.

"Mr. Horatio Silverton?"

The mortician blinked myopically though his spectacles and opened the door to his fine home a little wider. "Mr. Adams?"

"Yes," Clint said, removing his Stetson and noticing the mortician's moon-faced wife staring at him from the hallway. "Could I speak to you a few minutes in private?"

Silverton swallowed noisily. He was a tall, cadaverous man

who always wore a black suit, white shirt, and tall hat, all food-stained and years out of style. Silverton was in his late fifties, and no one knew where he had come from when the Comstock was discovered. But since murders were so frequent in western Nevada, Silverton had prospered. He'd opened a funeral parlor in Virginia City and made a considerable amount of money, then sold it to a younger man and moved down to Carson City, where the snow was not so deep in winter and the wind did not howl so fiercely.

"Uh . . . how can I help you?" he asked as he followed Clint out into his own yard, where not even a blade of grass grew because he was allergic to greenery.

"I was wondering what you found on the bodies of the outlaws," Clint said. "The one I shot in the street outside the bank and, most recently, the man that tried to assassinate me in Miss Butler's hallway."

Silverton removed a handkerchief from his coat pocket and mopped his brow. The man was very nervous; the afternoon was not at all hot.

"Uh . . . well, there was the usual," he said.

"Such as?"

"A little money. Barely enough to cover the funeral costs, of course."

Clint did not even try to hide his smile. "Of course. It's a great public service you and the men of your profession perform in the service of mankind. As a sheriff of some repute and experience, I well remember our own good mortician. He often buried the unworthy at his own expense. Like yourself, he was a very charitable man."

Silverton loosened up under Clint's praise. "Well," he said, visibly relaxing, "I'm certainly glad that someone understands. Our own sheriff has never once voiced his appreciation. And"— the mortician leaned closer and whispered, though there was no one around except themselves—"and if the sheriff reaches the deceased before I do, he has been known to steal the deceased's money!"

"Really!" Clint clucked his tongue and shook his head. "And he, a man sworn to uphold the law, stealing himself."

"Terrible, isn't it," the mortician said, getting warmed up to the subject. "And just the other day—"

"Tell me," Clint interrupted, "did either of Blackstone's men have anything written on their person?"

"You mean like a letter or something?"

"Yes, exactly! Or a receipt of some kind that might give me a clue where they banked, boarded their horses, or bought their meals. Anything at all."

The mortician smiled, for he was now eager to please this sympathetic exlawman.

"As a matter of fact, yes! The man you shot outside the bank had a letter, and the one you killed at Miss Butler's did have a few papers in his pocket. But I didn't pay them any attention. And the sheriff, well, he's too lazy and stupid to ask, so I just tossed them in my wastebasket."

"At your funeral parlor?"

"Yes."

"Then let's go see if they're still in the basket."

Protest flared in the mortician's eyes. "But I am just about to sit down and enjoy my supper with Mrs. Silverton."

Clint took the mortician's arm in a hard grip and jerked him in the direction of town. "Supper can wait just a little bit now, can't it?"

When the mortician looked into Clint's eyes, he damned well decided that supper with the missus could wait however long Clint liked.

NINE

As they walked up the main street of town, Clint saw Big Joe Gritts step out of the sheriff's office and watch. That galled Clint, because he knew full well that Gritts was going to be dogging his tracks, following up every lead he had and using Clint's considerable law experience to gather his own clues until he figured that he could find Harry Blackstone and kill the man for the ten-thousand-dollar reward.

"You see that huge sonofabitch across the street watching us?"

Silverton nodded.

"He's going to be asking you what I wanted in your office."

"I swear I won't say a thing."

"No," Clint said patiently, "you don't understand. I want you to tell him about the letters and things. You haven't read them yourself, have you?"

"Why of course not!"

"Good. Just tell that man that I picked the letter and other scraps of paper up. That will be the truth, and it just might bring him to me."

"But . . . but why should I tell him anything at all?" the mortician asked.

"Because," Clint said, "if you don't, he'd torture, then kill you."

Silverton looked as if he were going to faint, and Clint

actually had to grab the man's elbow and steady his gait as they walked the last few blocks to the funeral parlor.

The letter and the scraps of paper were tucked neatly into an envelope, and Clint did not bother to read them as he slipped the envelope into his coat pocket.

"Are you going to leave me?"

"Yes," Clint said.

"But . . . but that man! What if he doesn't believe me and hurts me? . . . Or worse?"

Clint frowned. "I tell you what," he said. "I'll leave and you stay. After I've traveled a block or two, I'll double back. Gritts ought to be in here by then, and if he gets rough, I'll step inside and get the drop on him. Given his criminal record, a simple assault charge will send him to the Nevada state prison, and that will be best for all of us."

But Silverton was not too wild about the idea. "It sounds like I'm to be bait! Really, Mr. Adams, the man could do me serious harm before you could intervene."

"Not likely," Clint said, wanting to reassure the mortician who looked frightened out of his mind. "You just tell him the truth: that I took a letter and several scraps of paper that you had removed from the outlaws' bodies. You don't have to say another damn thing."

Silverton pulled a handkerchief out of his coat pocket and nervously mopped his face. "Oh, how I wish you'd just left me out of this!"

"I'm sure you do," Clint said, "but maybe the things you've given me will help me track down Harry Blackstone and his men. If I do, you'll have done a great service to all law-abiding citizens, Mr. Silverton."

"But you'll get the entire reward and I'll have taken all the risks!"

"Hardly," Clint snapped, as he headed for the front door with his patience worn thin.

Gritts was standing in the shadows of an alley, and Clint pretended not to see him as he walked quickly up the street, then turned at the first block and waited. He did not have to wait long. Gritts was not a patient man, and he waited less than a minute before he emerged from the alley and headed across the street toward the funeral parlor.

Clint waited until the man had gone inside, then he started back. He very much hoped that Gritts would get rough with Silverton and give him the excuse he needed to make a citizen's arrest. Clint knew the local judge, and he was sure he could convince him to send Gritts to the state prison or at least give the outlaw-turned-bounty-hunter a long jail sentence.

Clint slipped up to the front door of the funeral parlor and listened for the cry of distress that would enable him to pull his six-gun and get the drop on Joe Gritts.

But the cry of pain never reached his ears, and although Clint could hear Gritt's deep, belligerent voice and Silverton's almost whining one, he could not detect that any violence was being committed.

Damn, he thought, as Gritts finished his business and came walking toward the door.

Clint stepped back and his hand automatically eased his six-gun up in his holster so that it rested light and easy. And when Gritts emerged in the doorway, Clint let him pass and then said, "Don't shadow me again or I'll drop you."

Gritts spun around in the street with amazing quickness and agility for a man who was at least six-foot-six and his hand flashed down to his gun, but when he saw Clint, he froze.

"Go ahead," Clint said, his own hand on his gun, which he was ready to draw. "Make your play, Joe. I figure that you mean to try and kill me, so why don't we settle this thing right here and now and be done with the fun and games?"

Gritts relaxed, and his hand moved away from the butt of

his gun. "Oh, no," he rumbled, "that would be playing to your advantage. You're a shade faster than I am. We both know that. So I think I'll just wait and kill you after you've led me to Harry Blackstone. I hear that you mean to get him for yourself. I guess there are probably ten good men running around looking for that reward, but it'll be either you or me that'll earn it."

"It'll be me, and you'll be pushing up daisies under Boot Hill while I spend the bounty," Clint said, wanting to goad the man into foolishness.

"Ha!" Gritts barked. "The trouble with you is that you've got a conscience. I ain't so encumbered. The last time we met, you were the lucky one and I got unlucky. But I've had years of prison to study on what happened and what won't happen the next time we have a showdown. And I'm gonna save all my planning as a big surprise."

"I'll bet it'll be a surprise all right," Clint said. "But mark my words, if I see you shadowing me again, I'll push you over the edge. I'll make you crawl in the dirt and bark like a dog if you won't draw on me face to face. You're too proud a man to be humiliated in front of a crowd. So you'll *have* to draw. It'll be a fair fight and I'll drill you like I should have the last time, instead of sending you to a prison so that you could be paroled and resume your murderous ways."

Gritts didn't like what Clint was saying at all, and in his heart he knew that the Gunsmith was right: His pride would not allow him to grovel, scrape, or bow before any man—even one who was fast enough with a gun to take his life.

"What if we buried the hatchet and worked together," Gritts said. "Blackstone has what—six, seven killers on his payroll. It's a two-man job. If we got ten thousand for Blackstone and two thousand apiece for his boys, that's twenty-two, maybe twenty-four thousand dollars. Split fifty-fifty, we'd both come out winners."

Clint laughed outright, and the giant flushed with embarrassment. "Well, goddamnit! It makes sense, don't it? We both could use some help against that many guns."

"I wouldn't trust you as far as I could throw you," Clint said slowly, "and that isn't very far. You'd use me, and then when the smoke cleared, you'd put a bullet in my back."

Gritts shook his head. "So I guess we'll just have to go our separate trails, and when we meet, we meet."

"That's right," Clint said.

"I don't suppose you'd be willing to tell me what that letter you got from the mortician says? Or those scraps of paper?"

"Gritts," said Clint, "you must have gotten feeble in the mind while you were doing all that thinking in prison. I won't tell you anything."

"Don't matter," Gritts said. "I already got some leads of my own. I'll find Blackstone before you do. When I do, I'll kill him and chop off his head so that no marshal or judge can say that I didn't earn the reward."

"Blackstone himself might have some trouble with that."

"He don't scare me. I think the man is crazy. Smart the way he and his men manage to disappear without a trace, but crazy-smart. Know what I mean?"

"Yeah," Clint said, "sort of like you."

Gritts shivered, and his hand dropped involuntarily toward his holster.

"Go on," Clint said, "draw."

Gritts shuddered again, but then he regained his control and started to turn away. "I'll pick my time."

"A man has a right to pick his own time to die," Clint said amiably. "I just hope you pick a time in the near future."

"You're too damn sure of yourself."

"I'm a very careful man," Clint said. "And I know when I've got the advantage on an overgrown maggot like you."

Gritts flushed with anger and he almost went for his gun,

which was exactly what Clint wanted. But instead, the man just turned away.

"Maybe later," Clint said as he turned on his boot heels and walked away from Gritts, wishing he'd have killed the man down in Texas and knowing the decision to capture him alive was going to cause him grief in Nevada and maybe even cost him his life.

Clint reached into his coat pocket and smoothed the letter between his thumb and forefinger. Hopefully the contents of that envelope would lead him straight to Harry Blackstone and his gang of cutthroats, thieves, and murderers.

TEN

Clint returned to Lucinda's house to get his things.

"Are you sure you have to go?" she asked.

Clint wavered. His intuition told him that if he pushed matters right this moment, he could have Lucinda in her bed. But Joe Gritts and Harry Blackstone were both after his hide, and he'd already decided that the farther away from Lucinda he could get, the safer she would be.

"Yeah," he said, "I have to go. But I'll be seeing you most every day. I mean to keep my shop open when I'm around, and I'll expect you to drop by whenever you see I'm open for business."

Lucinda came into his arms. "Clint," she said, "why don't we just go away together? Put this all behind us for a while? I'll . . . be yours, if that's what you want."

The heat from her body fired his blood, but he shook his head. "It's no good right now," he said, "and it won't be until I've settled with Blackstone and his gang of killers."

"Let someone else track them down," she pleaded. "If we were married, you wouldn't need the reward money. I've—"

Clint placed his fingers over her lips. "Uh-uh," he said gently. "I'd never be a kept man. And besides, I'm beginning to think that Blackstone is too clever to be caught by a bunch of amateurs. I've got to find him and put an end to his gang, Lucinda. It's just something I have to do—for your father, for

Agnes, and for this whole town."

Lucinda pulled away. She raised her chin and forced a smile. "I understand," she said, "and in a way, I'd be disappointed if you turned your back on those killers. But I just don't want you to get shot again."

"I'll be more careful," he promised, heading into her bedroom and gathering up his belongings.

On his way out, he kissed her good-bye and then he headed for the hotel in which he stayed.

The Sierra Hotel was a respectable establishment. It had six rooms on the bottom floor and seven on the top. Men only were permitted, and no drunken rowdiness or whores were allowed inside. Downstairs there was a small bar where one of the rooms had been converted, and the owner of the hotel was the man who poured the drinks. Jed Bacon was a quiet man who'd been crippled up in the Sierras in a mining accident.

Clint went into the little saloon and bought himself a beer—or at least he tried to buy himself a beer, but none of the other hotel patrons would give him the chance.

So he drank more than a few free beers while men crowded around and asked his opinion of the Blackstone Gang. Clint never said a word about the letter hidden inside his coat pocket or the scraps of paper that had been found on the dead outlaws' bodies by the town's mortician.

"I don't have any idea where they go and hide," Clint said. "One thing for sure: They are slick and they operate with a plan. They strike, make a big haul, and then vanish. To do that, I'm pretty sure that they split up and each go their separate ways."

"But it's Blackstone that everyone is after," a man said. "He's the one that's behind everything."

"Sure he is," Clint said. "And that's why I'm setting my sights on him. Besides, he'll be the one that has most of your money."

"If you don't get it back, you bet the damned sheriff sure won't," a man groused.

"That's right," several others said, jumping into the conversation to state their disgust for Sheriff Williamson and his inept efforts to gain some lead on the case. "I don't see why we don't dump the fat sonofabitch come the next election. Hell, we'll double the salary and hire Clint!"

"Oh no you don't," Clint said when everyone began to cheer. "I've got a gunsmithing business now."

"Aw hell," a man said, "you're good at that, but you're never in the shop! You're either out squiring Miss Butler around or else fishing down along the Carson River."

Clint had to smile, because there was more than a little truth in what the man was saying. "Well," he vowed, "as soon as I see Blackstone and his gang either swing from a rope or marched into prison, then I'll keep more regular hours."

None of them believed him, and before they could hoorah Clint anymore, he gathered up his saddlebags and headed upstairs to his room.

It wasn't much of a room—just ten by ten square—but it had a window and curtains, and the bed was soft and the sheets were changed once a week by a Chinese man whose wife cleaned the room every other Tuesday.

Clint tossed his saddlebags down on his bed and locked the door behind him. Then he pulled the letter and scraps of paper he'd gotten from the undertaker and sat down on the bed to see if he had some real clues as to the identity of the killers.

The letter was addressed to "William" and it was from the man's brother, announcing his decision to come to Virginia City to work in the mines or, better yet, in some "more remunerative occupation better suited to my talents." The letter gave the expected time of arrival by stage in Virginia City and was signed by "Andrew Underwood, Esquire."

Clint frowned with disappointment, because the letter of-

fered no clue whatsoever to William's identity. Clint noted that
the stage was due in the next day and decided that, even though
it was a very long shot, he had better at least meet the stage and
see what Mr. Underwood could tell him about his brother's
activities. Most likely he probably didn't even know that his
brother was a member of the infamous Blackstone Gang.

The other scraps of paper he had obtained from the mortician
were also disappointing. One was a ticket from, of all places,
Piper's Opera House. This was surprising, since it had not been
Clint's experience that outlaws were long on cultural events.
But then neither were Western sheriffs like himself known to
be patrons of the arts.

There was also a laundry ticket, but the establishment's
name was washed out so that it could not be deciphered. The
other scraps of paper yielded even less information. Just a few
receipts, a scrap of paper from a tobacco advertisement, and
finally, a receipt for $57.50 for a roan horse.

Clint frowned. Maybe on his way up Gold Canyon through
Silver City and Gold Hill he would stop at the liveries and see
if he could find out which one had sold a rather valuable roan
horse for that exact amount of money. If he could do that, then
perhaps the seller would also remember a few other valuable
bits of useful information.

Anything, Clint thought, because I've got nothing to go on
but what little I've learned from this letter and scrap of paper.

The next morning, Clint went to his own livery and had his
black gelding, Duke, saddled.

"Nice day for a ride," the liveryman said, "but you look a
might peeky to be riding so soon after getting shot."

"The fresh air will do me good, and I'll take it nice and
slow," Clint said, grunting with pain as he pulled himself up
into the saddle.

He traveled east along a very well-used road that was already busy with freight traffic. After topping some low hills, the road suddenly turned north and began to climb up the rough, barren hills toward the famed Comstock Lode.

The farther he went, the more congested became the freight traffic. A steady stream of huge and high-sided ore wagons rolled down toward the Carson River, where the smelting mills churned out a constant stream of smoke. Other wagons pulled by as many as sixteen mules or horses labored up the steep grade, pulling heavy loads of supplies, machinery, and shoring timber for the deep, hard-rock mines and the miners who worked them.

Clint and Duke had to keep edging over to the side of the road lest they be run over by the swearing, whip-snapping freighters who seemed to figure that they alone had the right of way.

When he finally reached Silver City, Clint visited the two livery stables and inquired about the roan horse but came up without any answers. He was not discouraged. There were several more liveries in Gold Hill and at least half a dozen up in Virginia City. He was sure that a roan horse worth the princely sum of $57.50 would be remembered. Most average saddle horses were going for no more than thirty dollars in western Nevada, where mustangs were plentiful and free for the catching and breaking.

In Gold Hill, he got lucky.

"Yeah," the liveryman said, examining the receipt Clint showed him, "I sold a roan for that amount. And sure, that's my receipt. But I won't take the horse back, and if he went lame, then—"

"That's not my problem," Clint said. "I'm just looking for the man who bought the horse. You remember anything about him?"

The liveryman frowned. "Let me see. Yeah, he was tall and had a funny way of talking."

"Funny? How?"

"I don't know. He spoke real . . . well, educated, like. He rolled his words and seemed to think a hell of a lot of himself. I got the feeling he was used to being a big deal or something."

"I see. Did he give you a name? Or where he lived or anything?"

"Just the money. And since it was good, I didn't see much point in asking. Which brings me to the question: Why all the questions?"

Clint remounted Duke. "No special reason, except that I'd like to meet the man. Do you see him ride by very often?"

"Now and then."

"Heading which way?"

"Sometimes up this canyon, sometimes down."

"Thanks," Clint said, feeling a little discouraged. "Appreciate your help."

"If you find him and he wants his money back, you tell him I spent it."

"I'll do that," Clint said as he rode away, hoping he'd have better luck in Virginia City with a young man coming in on the afternoon stage.

ELEVEN

When Clint rode over the Divide into Virginia City, he reined Duke aside for a blow after the long, hard climb up to the Comstock Lode. Besides his horse needing a breather, Clint enjoyed this first majestic view of Virginia City.

To the west towered mighty Sun Mountain, which cast its giant shadow over Virginia City and was a landmark that could be seen for a hundred miles. On the mountain's barren slopes were thousands of miners working their little claims, and at each one you could see a pile of yellow- and rust-colored tailings. The city itself was the second largest in the West, with a bustling population of more than eighteen thousand.

Virginia Street teemed with miners, freighters, Chinamen, and Indians, all hustling to make their fortunes off the fabulous ore bodies that lay buried hundreds of feet below the surface. There were dozens of saloons and about every kind of shop and establishment a man could want. The red-light district was a major attraction, and Clint had heard that some of the higher-class prostitutes were asking and getting as much as ten dollars a tumble.

Money flowed in Virginia City, even if the water was bad and the climate even worse. Up here, a man froze in the winter when the infamous Washoe Zephyr blew like a hurricane. At such times, immense clouds of dust would obliterate the town and fill everyone's lungs with grit and dirt. In the winter blizzards were not uncommon, and in the summer the days were so scorching hot the sun seemed to fry the rocks. There were no trees, not even the scrubby little pinion and juniper pines. Even those had been used up for firewood.

Clint marveled at the sight that stretched out before him: the huge mines with their avalanche-sized tailings and plumes of smoke rising up from the great, pounding stamp mills; the colossal tin buildings that housed tens of thousands of dollars worth of heavy machinery that was systematically eating away at the Comstock, hungry for its fabulous treasures of silver and gold; the Virginia and Truckee Railroad and its bustling train station just below the town; the hundreds of tents, shacks, and even mansions of the rich that dotted the landscape.

"If Harry Blackstone and his gang are here, they're going to be the devil to dig out," Clint said to his horse.

In answer, Duke shook his head and his glossy black mane waved in the breeze. Clint touched the animal's sweaty neck, judged that he had cooled down enough, and urged him into the heavy traffic that wound its way into the city.

Clint's first stop was the stagecoach office. "When does your next stage arrive?"

"From where?"

Clint pulled the letter out of his pocket and looked at the postmark. "From Chicago."

"That'd be from all points east," the ticket agent said with an air of boredom.

"Fine. When does it arrive?"

"Two already have. Two more are due in before midnight."

Clint shook his head. It had not occurred to him that there would be so many stages arriving in a single day.

"Have you seen a young man arrive asking for his brother?"

"Of course not," the agent snapped. "I have no interest or concern in such matters. My sole purpose for being behind this ticket counter is to sell tickets for the Comstock Stagecoach Company."

Clint reached across the counter and grabbed the man's prominent nose between his middle and forefingers, then yanked on it hard.

"Ouch!" the agent cried, grabbing at his nose. "Damn you! I'll have you—"

The agent did not have a chance to finish, as Clint's fist exploded against his jaw, sending him backward to crash into the wall. The agent's eyes turned glassy, and he slid down to the floor and did not move.

"Serves the mouthy ticket agent right," a young man said, coming up to stand beside Clint. "I asked him if he knew my brother and he insulted me. I should have given him the same dose of manners that you just did."

Clint turned to see a tall, handsome young man of about twenty, with sandy hair, blue eyes, and broad shoulders. "Would you be Andrew Underwood?"

"Why, yes sir!"

Underwood stuck out his hand, and although his grip was powerful, the hand was soft. Whatever Underwood had done in Chicago, it was not manual labor. "Are you a friend of my brother?"

Clint had a difficult moment. He should have already worked up some explanation, but he hadn't. "Not exactly," he said. "In fact . . . well, why don't we go have a beer and I'll explain."

"Well, I can't do that." Underwood's smile faded. He had a square jaw and strong features. "I'd better wait for my brother. His name is William."

"Yes," Clint said, "I understand that. It's why I'm here."

"You looking for him, too?"

"Not exactly," Clint said, taking the man's arm and steering him out the door.

"Now wait a minute," Underwood protested. "I've got my bags still stacked inside and—"

"Maybe we'd better get them," Clint said, reversing direction.

"That's them over there against the wall."

There were two big trunks and a suitcase. "All that?" Clint asked.

"Why sure!" Underwood shrugged. "It's everything I own in this world. I came out West intending to stay."

"I can see that," Clint said. He picked the smaller trunk and stooped over to grab it. The damn thing was heavy, and when he tried to lift it, the bullet wound in his side felt as if someone had jabbed it with a red-hot poker.

"Uhhh," Clint groaned, releasing his grip and straightening his back.

"What's the matter!"

"I got a little bullet wound in my side," Clint explained. "I'm afraid that if I try to lift that thing, I'll reopen it."

"You picked the one with my books," Underwood said, grabbing the trunk and tossing it up onto his wide shoulders. Then he grabbed the other trunk by one handle and picked it up. "The suitcase is real light. If you could manage that, I'd be grateful."

Clint nodded weakly. He was impressed with Andrew Underwood's tremendous strength. The trunk of books had to weigh at least ninety pounds, and the man had snatched it up as if it were a shoe box, while the big trunk looked like it would weigh no less than forty or fifty pounds empty.

Clint carefully picked up the suitcase. It wasn't heavy, but it wasn't all that light, either.

"Where are we going?" Underwood asked.

"Beats me."

"Well, aren't you taking me to my brother?"

"I don't think so," Clint said, as he started toward the nearest hotel, where he figured they could dump the luggage and then find a quiet place to talk.

A pair of loud crashes brought Clint around, and he saw that Underwood had dumped both trunks on the boardwalk, planted his feet down solidly, and placed his hands on his narrow hips.

"What's the matter?"

"I'm not following some stranger up and down the street without knowing why," Underwood said, the muscles in his jaw cording like cables.

Clint could appreciate the man's position but not his timing. "We need to talk in private," he said.

"About my brother?"

"Yes."

"Where is he?"

Clint sighed. "He's resting in the cemetery at Carson City."

Underwood paled. His hand involuntarily lifted to cross his eyes, as if he could wipe away this piece of hard news. Clint set the suitcase down in an alley between two stores and motioned for Underwood to drag the trunks in as well.

"Listen," he said, taking the younger man's arm as they stepped off the crowded boardwalk filled with miners, "I didn't want to tell you this on the street, but your brother was killed in a bank holdup early last week."

"Bank robbers shot him!"

Clint took a deep breath. He didn't know how Underwood was going to take this news, and he sure didn't want to wrestle with the powerful young man. "Not exactly."

"What do you mean?"

"I . . . I had to shoot him," Clint said in a quiet voice.

Underwood lunged at Clint but the Gunsmith, anticipating this, had already reached for his six-gun, and it came up faster than the strike of a rattlesnake. Clint cocked it in one smooth motion, and it came to rest exactly at a point between Underwood's eyes.

The young man from Chicago froze. His blue eyes met in the middle and fixed on the gun barrel.

"Now," Clint said quietly, "why don't you sit down and let me tell you the rest of it."

Underwood sat down in the dirt of the alley and swallowed. He was afraid, but it was anger that was causing him to tremble.

"You better tell me everything, mister," he hissed, "because my brother William was a damn good man!"

Clint chose his words carefully. "I don't know what kind of a man he was, Andrew. The sad truth of the matter is that the West turns a lot of good men bad. They arrive out here without friends or family and often without any money. The work is deadly and hard in the Comstock mines. Faced with the daily chance of being buried alive in a cave-in, or shot off the seat of a stagecoach, or knifed in a card game, they sometimes chose the easy money."

"Not William!"

Clint kept his gun trained on the younger man. "Sometimes they're even blackmailed or tricked into doing unlawful things. It could be that your brother got into debt and Harry Blackstone offered him what he thought was a safe, easy way out."

"Who's Harry Blackstone?" Underwood demanded.

"It was his gang that robbed the bank in Carson City. Blackstone is the leader, and he's been robbing and killing in these parts for months. Anyway, the man cut the bank manager's throat and left him gagging to die in his own blood."

Clint read faces well, and when he saw the shock in Underwood's eyes, he lowered his gun and eased down the hammer. "Yeah," Clint said, "and if you don't believe me, you can come on down to Carson City and ask questions. Not only were the bank manager and two others killed, but a woman had her skull fractured in a pistol whipping. She was my friend, Andrew. A good, decent woman who probably tried to interfere and was beaten to death."

Underwood began to shake his head. "My brother would never have done anything like that. Never!"

"There were six of them," Clint said, "so it's plenty likely you are right. Let's give your brother the benefit of the doubt. But the fact remains that he was a member of the Blackstone Gang that day, and when the bullets were flying, he caught mine. I didn't have time to pick and choose my targets. I just tried to save my life and take theirs."

Underwood expelled a long, deep breath, and he scrubbed his face with both hands. "We were raised in a Christian family," he whispered, "though Father was a hard man and plenty willing to give us a hiding."

Clint reached out and patted the man on the shoulder. "I'm sorry you came all the way out here to find this out. It might have been better if I'd lied to you about your brother, but that isn't my style."

"I almost wish you had," the young man said. "William was my idol when we were growing up in Chicago. He fought bigger kids to protect me, and I worshiped the ground he walked upon."

Clint stood up. He didn't know what to say. "Have you got enough money to go back home?"

"I'm not going home," Underwood said, coming to his feet.

"There's nothing for you here. I got your letter from the mortician in Carson City. That's how I came to be here today. But you'd sure be wiser to go home now instead of working in the mines. That's a terrible way to earn your keep."

"Then I'll find something else to do," Underwood said with determination. "I may teach school."

"The school year is already underway," Clint said, "and most people favor ladies for that kind of work."

Underwood shook his head. "Then I'll work for the newspaper. Yes, that's what I'll do! I'm a fine writer. I've had a decent education."

Clint shrugged. "I could introduce you at the *Territorial Enterprise*. It's run by Dan DeQuille, one of the best journalists I ever read. He works with another talented writer, a man that signs his prose 'Mark Twain.' "

"Funny name," Underwood said.

"He's a very funny man," Clint said. "Down in Carson City, his humor is the only thing that sells the paper. We have our own newspaper, but you don't find the kind of talent that DeQuille and Twain bring to the page very often."

"Well," Underwood said, "it sounds like I might be out of my league, but I'll have a talk with them. I come too far to go back now. I mean to find out the reason why my brother joined an outlaw gang. I won't rest until I know all the sad circumstances of his death."

"I understand that," Clint said. "And I want you to know I'm sorry he was your brother. I'm also tracking down every lead I can dig up on the Blackstone Gang. But so far, I haven't had much to go on. You obviously don't know anything that could help me."

"Such as?"

"Did your brother speak in a refined voice? An unusual voice?"

Underwood stared at him. "Why, yes, he did. How did you know that? Did he say something before he died?"

"No," Clint said, "he bought a good roan horse, and the man who sold it to him remarked on your brother's voice. But yours isn't unusual—why . . . "

"William fancied himself a Shakespearean actor of some merit," Underwood said. "He used to recite Shakespeare every waking hour. He'd roll his words and mimic the voices of every great actor he'd heard on stage."

Clint's eyes widened. "Piper's Opera House," he whispered.

"What?"

"Never mind."

"No!" Underwood exclaimed. "If what I've just revealed has somehow given you a clue about the gang and my brother's involvement, then I want to know about it. I *demand* to know about it!"

Young Underwood looked plenty serious as he blocked Clint's path back to the alley. And while the Gunsmith could have easily pistol-whipped the Easterner, he had to admire his spunk.

"Why don't we find you a hotel room, and then we'll pay a visit to Piper's Opera House. If your brother loved the stage, then he would have been a frequent visitor there."

"All right," Underwood said, scooping up both trunks with ease, "let's go."

As they walked along, men moved aside for them: Underwood just had the look of a very formidable opponent, and Clint shared that same impression with his lean, easy, but confident stride.

They found a clean enough hotel for three dollars a week and deposited Underwood's belongings before they left to pay Piper's Opera House a visit.

"Just one rule," Clint said. "I do all the talking. I've been a lawman for a number of years and I know how to dig for information. But you come on too strong, and people either clam up or they get testy."

"I'll be quiet," Underwood promised, "unless I get the impression someone is trying to hide something from me about William."

Clint glanced sideways at his big friend. He was not at all sure he should not have ditched the man from Chicago at once.

"Here's the *Territorial Enterprise* offices," he said, coming to a halt. "Why don't we go inside and I'll introduce you? Then . . ."

"Later," said Underwood. "First let's find out about my brother."

Clint frowned. "All right," he said, "but just remember to keep your mouth shut and your ears wide open."

"You sure are one to hand out a lot of advice," Underwood snorted.

"May be, but there's four dead people besides your brother who have died in my town, and I mean to stop at nothing to catch Harry Blackstone and bring his entire gang to justice."

"I feel the exact same way."

"It doesn't matter how you feel," Clint said bluntly. "You're not a lawman, and you've probably never even handled a gun."

"You got that much right," Underwood said, "but before this day is over, I'm going to buy one, along with a whole lot of ammunition. And I'll practice every spare minute I have."

"Why?"

"Because I mean to kill this Blackstone if I can," Underwood replied. "To my way of thinking, *he's* the one that killed my brother, not you."

"That's a great comfort," Clint said. "But you're out of your element here. Besides, there are half a dozen men who are already trying to earn the bounty on Blackstone and his gang."

"Is it offered dead or alive?"

"Yep."

"How much?"

Clint told him.

"Good," said Underwood, "with that kind of money, I can tell Mr. DeQuille to shove his inkwell up his ass if he gives me a bad time."

Despite the grim situation, Clint had to grin as he walked along. "Are all men from Chicago as tough and determined as you?"

"Most are," Underwood said. "Especially those of us that come from poor, God-fearing families. I was taught the Scripture, and it reads 'an eye for an eye and a tooth for a tooth.'"

Underwood looked sideways at Clint. "Christian charity is a fine thing, but I lost the only brother I had because of an outlaw leader named Harry Blackstone. I'm not one to accept that sort of thing without payback."

Clint stopped in his tracks. "Listen," he said, "besides me, there really are dozens of bounty hunters racing all over this part of the country, trying to turn over any stone that will lead them to the Blackstone Gang and that reward money. And one of those men is Big Joe Gritts. He's a cold-blooded killer in his own right, and he'd eat a young fellow like you up and spit him out without working up a sweat."

"You tell me what he looks like," Underwood said, "and I'll see that I hit him before he hits me."

Clint shook his head. Underwood was a very confident young man but also an ignorant one. And ignorance coupled with confidence usually spells a bad ending.

TWELVE

Piper's Opera House had already been burned to the ground once but was immediately rebuilt to its former state of elegance and grandeur. An immense, two-story building, its cavernous interior boasted one of the biggest and finest stages in the entire country, being over fifty feet wide and thirty feet deep. There were suspended box seats of the type that Clint would have rented for five dollars on the night he was to escort Lucinda, a dress circle where the seats ran one dollar, and what was called the "pigpen" located farther out from the stage, where the rough and coarse miners could spit and stomp and enjoy themselves for just four bits a performance.

As Clint and Underwood entered the now empty building, they read on the marquee that that night's performance would begin with a singer named Willowby Williams, followed by a recital from *Hamlet*, followed by a minstrel show, and the closing finale was to be a cockfight, cocks supplied by Henry Gonzales and Peter Dent.

"Sounds interesting to me," Underwood said, rolling his eyes in amazement.

"The crowds up here will tolerate anything but being bored," Clint said. "And if the entertainment drags, they'll usually turn upon each other and start brawling."

Underwood shook his head, and as they started across the

vast hardwood floor, he stopped and turned with a question on his face. "Feels strange."

"The floor is suspended over railroad springs," Clint explained. "Sometimes at a dance they will get six or seven hundred drunken miners in here to bounce up and down. It's quite a sight and experience to feel the entire floor rocking."

"I'll bet," Underwood said.

"May I help you gentlemen? We are closed until seven o'clock tonight, when we have a wonderful show. So if you'll simply be kind enough to leave and return later, I would be most grateful."

Clint recognized the short, bald man with the reddish goatee as John Piper, owner and proprietor of the establishment.

"Mr. Piper," he said, taking off his hat. "My name is Clint Adams, and this is my friend Andrew Underwood."

Both extended their hands.

"Adams. Adams," Piper repeated, cocking his head to the side. "Your name is very familiar, but I can't place your face, sir."

"That's because we've never met before. But I am a gunsmith down in Carson City and—"

"You are *the* Gunsmith!" Piper exclaimed. "Of course! You, sir, are reputed to be the fastest gun in the entire West!"

"Not likely," Clint said, feeling his cheeks warm with embarrassment.

"Of course you are!" Piper said, pumping his hand energetically. "You are a genuine legend! Sir, this is a great honor. I wonder if I might employ your talents."

Underwood was looking at Clint strangely, as if seeing him for the very first time.

"I would be more than willing," Piper was saying, "to pay you, say, fifty dollars for each shooting exhibition you perform. That would, of course, include a speech about the most famous desperadoes you have gunned down during your long and illustrious law career."

"I'm afraid I'm not interested," Clint said, noting the iciness that had crept into Underwood's eyes.

"Then how about seventy-five dollars a night! That's much more than a month's wages on the Comstock. Easy money to be had, and I might even be able to increase the payment if your appearances draw the expected crowds."

"Mr. Piper," Clint said, "I'm sorry, but the last thing I want to do is to stand up on that stage and tell a bunch of drunken miners about the men I've had to kill during my law career. Now, the reason I came was to ask you if you knew a man named William."

Piper was not pleased by Clint's refusal or the switching of their topic of conversation. "I know dozens—no, *hundreds* of Williams," he groused. "So what?"

Underwood stepped in. "He was my brother and he was killed in a holdup attempt in Carson City. He was a member of Harry Blackstone's Gang, and—"

"I said I'd do the talking," Clint snapped.

Piper shook his head. "Neither one of you has bothered to tell me what in the world all of this has to do with me and this opera house."

"Just this," Clint said, "his brother was a thespian. His name was William Underwood, and I'm sure he would have been a regular patron."

"Then I wish I'd have know that!" Piper crowed. "We could have hired him as an attraction! A *curiosity*!"

"Please," Underwood said, "if you knew him, perhaps you could help us understand why he joined the Blackstone Gang."

Piper threw up his hands in a gesture of futility. "To begin with, I am not acquainted with anyone named Underwood. And second, only a fool would have used his real name if he intended to join a gang. So why are you wasting my time? Was your brother an identical twin?"

"No."

"Then I cannot be of any help to you whatsoever."

Piper started to turn away, but Clint grabbed his sleeve. "Sir, one more moment, please. Any help you can provide will save lives and end the reign of terror that Blackstone is inflicting on this part of Nevada. This man was an actor. Even if he used an alias—and I'm sure that you are correct in saying he did—he had a stage voice. And . . . and he rode a fine roan horse."

Piper yanked his sleeve from Clint's grip. "I have dozens of actors come by each week seeking work. Most of them are actors in name only and I send them on their way after a brief audition. I hire almost exclusively traveling troupes of actors. Local talent is almost always bad talent."

"My brother was gifted," Underwood said angrily.

Piper snorted with contempt. "If he was so 'gifted' then why would he join a gand of merciless killers?"

Clint saw something flare in Underwood's eyes and he grabbed him before he could reach the smaller man.

"We'll be leaving," Clint said, forcibly shoving Underwood toward the exit.

"Good! That's what I requested from the start. But Mr. Adams?"

Clint was at the door, shoving Underwood outside, when he heard the voice and turned back. "Yes?"

"What about we start at one hundred dollars? I am sure you can draw nearly eight hundred spectators and—"

"Not interested at any price."

Piper's lower lip curled so that his beard lifted like the hair on a dog's back. "Then you, sir, are a fool."

"Oh, I've always suspected that, and my friends have known it as a fact for a good many years now. But somehow I just keep fumbling along through life. And I'm doing just fine without joining your menagerie, thank you very kindly."

Piper stomped his heel down hard on the hardwood floor and the sound of it echoed throughout the great hall. "On second thought, *don't* come back for tonight's performance."

"With a lineup like you've got in store, you can bet I won't," Clint said as he turned and went back outside.

Underwood was fuming. "So what do we do now?"

" 'We' don't do anything," Clint said. "I showed you where the *Territorial Enterprise* office was. Either go get a job or go back to the stageline and buy yourself a return ticket to Chicago."

"I'm not going to do either," Underwood said. "I'm going man hunting with you."

"What!"

"You heard me."

"I won't have it!" Clint stormed.

"I'll follow you everywhere you go."

"I won't have that either."

"Then," said Underwood with dead seriousness, "you'll have to kill me. Because we are talking about the death of my only brother. And I'm not resting until I know why he joined that gang. Now, I assume he left a Colt, a horse, and a saddle."

Clint frowned. "He did."

"So where are they?"

"In Carson City."

"Where you are heading, right?"

"That's right, but—"

"Then I hope your horse rides double."

"He doesn't."

"Then I'll either take a stagecoach or the railroad down to Carson City. And you can tell whoever has my brother's horse and gun and whatever else he had in his possession when he died that I will be along shortly."

Clint knew that he was beaten. "All right," he said, "the

sheriff has your brother's things. The town would auction off the horse and belongings if they weren't claimed, but generally, the sheriff sort of manages to lose a few things."

"Then I must see him at once."

"Let's go then," Clint said wearily. "The way you operate, you'd probably antagonize Sheriff Williamson and get thrown in his jail—or worse."

Underwood fell in beside the Gunsmith. They were both silent and grim as they walked back to the hotel.

"I've decided not to stay," Underwood told the hotel's proprietor. "I'd like my three dollars back, please."

"Sorry. No refunds."

Underwood looked at Clint. "Is this standard practice?"

"Not that I know of."

"That's what I thought," Underwood said as his hand shot across the registration desk, and he grabbed the man's nose between his bent forefingers and yanked it so hard the man bellowed in pain.

"All right! All right! You can have your damn three dollars back! But let go of my nose!"

Underwood released the man, who was so hurt and furious that he began to curse them both. Underwood's knuckles killed the cursing as they broke through the hotel man's front teeth and lips. The man crashed up against his pigeonhole filing box, and then he slid down to the floor with his eyes rolling up into his head.

"You were pretty rough on him," Clint said as Underwood stepped behind the desk and rifled the drawer until he found the money and extracted his three dollars.

"You set a good example over at the stagecoach line," said Underwood. "I'll get my trunks and we'll leave at once."

"My horse won't ride double and carry those damn trunks."

"Then we'll rent a buckboard or whatever you call them. I'll use the three dollars on it. Fair enough?"

Clint watched the young man bound up the stairs and disappear.

"Fair enough," he said with a shake of his head.

Clint walked back into town and untied his horse. He supposed the best thing to do was to keep the young Easterner close for a while until the fool realized that a man could and would get himself killed in the West if he poked his nose into business that he did not understand.

"Hell," Clint groused out loud, "as if I don't have enough problems already."

THIRTEEN

The buckboard ride down to Carson City was enjoyable enough. Clint tied Duke to the wagon and drove while Underwood stared in amazement at all the mining activity.

"I can see that some people are getting very rich," he said, pointing to a huge mansion, "but most of the miners are damn poor."

"That's right," Clint said. "I know very little about mining, but what I can say is that many of the miners here came over from the Sierras after the California Gold Rush petered out. You'll see a lot of old Forty-Niners up here."

"That great ore strike happened before I was even born!"

"I was just a little kid myself," Clint said. "Anyway, in the Sierras, a man could stand a fair chance of making a strike if he had nothing more than luck, pluck, and a mining pan. But not here."

"Why not?"

"Because in California it was all placer mining. The gold was right on the surface—usually in the streams. But up here on the Comstock, it's all deep underground. The veins of gold and silver are tilted up on end, like those hanging file folders in an office desk."

"Huh," Underwood grunted, "so all the mining is mostly underground."

"That's right. Deep underground. Some of the bigger mines

like the Savage and the Consolidated are tunneling out of shafts that run a thousand feet underground. They tell me the temperatures down there run to well over a hundred degrees."

"A real hell that must be."

"Exactly," Clint said.

Underwood pointed up toward the hundreds of little tailings, each signifying a claim. "If what you say is true about the ore being so deep underground, why are all those little shafts being worked with a pick and shovel?"

"Good question," Clint said. "I guess the answer is that now and then, an outcropping of the big underground veins will rise up close to the surface, where it can be tapped without digging more than ten or twenty feet underground. That only has to occur once or twice to send all the miners digging like gophers in the hope that their little claims are resting just over the same outcropping. A lot of those claims are worked by men during their off-duty hours with the big mines."

Underwood shook his head. "What do the 'big mines' pay for sending men into a living hell?"

"Three dollars a day, but the union is pushing for five."

"That's a lot of money. Back in Chicago, working men make about twenty cents an hour."

"Nobody working a pick or shovel is getting rich up here," Clint pointed out. "Prices, as you come to learn, are damned high. Besides that, the miners spend their wages as soon as they get paid, usually on liquor and women. It's a hard life, and the pleasures outside of whores and whiskey are few."

"I never planned to be a miner anyway," Underwood said. "I didn't get educated to work underground like a varmint."

"What kind of books are packed in that trunk that damn near broke my back?"

"Law books, mostly."

Clint groaned. "Not another lawyer! Hell, they're crawling

all over the place up here, trying to suck off everyone's profits. Now, if you were a doctor . . . that would be different. There aren't enough of them to go around."

"Well," said Underwood, "I'm not a doctor, and if what you say about the legal profession is true, then I'll pass on that as well. I guess, to be honest, I'd prefer to be a journalist anyway. Perhaps even a novelist."

"Now that would be a good profession, if it payed. And let me tell you something, Andrew: There is a lot to write about up here."

The younger man smiled. "Perhaps I'll write about how we apprehended the murderous Blackstone Gang."

"I hope I live to see you write about it," Clint said. "The man has sworn to kill me—if Big Joe Gritts doesn't ambush me first."

"You can definitely use a partner," Underwood said. "And the moment we reach Carson City, I shall make it a point to buy a serviceable revolver and plenty of ammunition. In a week or two—"

Clint had to laugh out loud. "Andrew," he said, "no offense, but I've spent years perfecting the draw and shoot. And around these parts, most of the men who carry a gun have worn it since they were knee-high to a jackrabbit. You'd have a lot of catching up to do. My advice would be to arm yourself with a hide-out gun."

"A hide-out gun?"

"A derringer," Clint explained. "You wear it hidden. That way, no drunken miner will see a hogleg like I'm wearing strapped around your waist and want to draw down on you. And with a hide-out, the idea is to use it only in self-defense. They're not generally accurate beyond the range of twenty or thirty feet."

"Then I'll buy one of them," Underwood decided out loud. "But I also fully intend to become proficient on the 'draw and shoot,' as you put it, and I'll wear a 'hogleg' like yours."

"Suit yourself," Clint said. "I've got a few used and re-worked pistols you might be interested in buying. I'm a gunsmith by trade."

"I thought you were a famous sheriff."

"I was a sheriff, but I found gunsmithing to be a healthier profession."

Underwood smiled. "Makes sense to me. And if your prices are right, then I'll buy both the hide-out and Derringer from you and begin practicing this very evening."

Clint expelled a deep breath. Andrew Underwood was sure a man with a stubborn mind. Clint still thought the best and safest thing the Easterner could do was to return to Chicago before he stepped on someone's toes and got himself ventilated.

Clint glanced up to see that they were approaching Devil's Gate, a high, narrow place in the canyon where some money-grubbing bunch had erected a toll gate for all the wagons passing through.

"Generally, I ride Duke on through and most of the men on foot hike around to the other canyon," he said. "It burns me to pay a toll. Whoever bought this piece of the canyon didn't do a damn thing to improve this wagon road. Doesn't seem right that they should gouge every wagon passing by."

"Then don't pay them," Underwood said in a bland voice. "I wouldn't."

"I never drove a wagon through here before," Clint said. "We'll see how much they want from us. If it's four bits or less, I'd rather pay than make trouble. I've problems enough right now without adding on anymore."

Underwood's blue eyes lifted toward the two riflemen stationed high up above. "Maybe you got a point," he said, "because it looks to me like these people are prepared to enforce their toll."

When Clint reached the gate, two rough-looking men sized

him up, and the taller one growled, "That'll be a dollar . . . each."

"What!"

"You heard him," the shorter one said. "We ain't standing here all day for nothing."

Clint burned inside. "This is highway robbery."

"It's the way it is, mister. You don't like it or you don't have two dollars, just turn that rig around and head on back up to the Comstock Lode. You can take the road down Six Mile Canyon for free."

"It's thirty miles out of my way to Carson City."

"Then you have a decision to make," the taller gunman said. "Is it worth your time to save two dollars—or not?"

"It's not," Clint said, giving the impression of reaching for his money but instead drawing his six-gun and pointing it at the man's face. "In fact," he added, "it's not worth it at all. Now it's *you* boys who have the decision to make."

The pair blinked with astonishment. Their cheeks flamed, and the smaller one looked like a puffed-up horned toad.

"Didn't you see those riflemen up above?" the taller man hissed. "They've got their Winchesters pointed right down on your head."

"I'm sure they do," Clint said, "but they can't see my gun pointed in your face. So either you act like I've paid and let us pass on through free, or else make a play and die."

"You'll both never live to drive that buckboard five feet!" the shorter man snorted.

"You won't know that," Clint said, "because you'll be dead before I will. Think about it."

The two gunmen did think about it real hard. They glanced up at their friends with the rifles but were smart enough to realize they'd be signing their own death warrants if they commanded the riflemen to open fire.

"I'm getting impatient waiting," Clint said.

"So am I," Underwood added.

"Get on by then!" the taller gunman choked, "but don't you ever plan on getting through here again. Either of you!"

"We'll most likely have to sooner or later," Clint said, "and when we do, you'd better be real polite and pass us through free or you're both dead men."

"Who the hell do you think you are, anyway!" the shorter man squealed.

"The Gunsmith," Clint said.

The two guards gaped at Clint and then they exchanged worried glances. "Mr. Adams, you just go right on ahead," the taller one said, "and you and your friend can pass through free if you want. We didn't know it was you."

Clint drove on through.

"I am damned impressed!" Underwood exclaimed. "Just your name alone seems to have put the fear of God in them. Is that what being the best with a six-gun gets a man in the West?"

"No," Clint said, "most often it gets him a cheap pine box and six feet of Boot Hill."

"Oh," the man from Chicago said, but his eyes still shone at Clint with admiration.

FOURTEEN

When they arrived back in Carson City, Clint drove the buckboard and livery horse over to an agreed-upon dropping-off place, and after returning Duke to his stall, he and Underwood walked up the street to the sheriff's office.

"Just let me handle this," Clint instructed. "The sheriff isn't too friendly, and he won't be one damn bit pleased when he learns that you want to claim your brother's belongings."

"To hell with him!" Underwood said.

"Fine, but just keep that sentiment to yourself. I'm not exactly bosom buddies with Williamson, but I sure don't want to prod the man into trying to arrest me."

"Would you allow it?"

"I don't know," Clint said. "The law is the law. I spent too many years trying to enforce it to trample on it now, even if it is being enforced by a man that I don't respect."

Underwood said nothing as they entered the office and, to Clint's amazement, almost ran right into Big Joe Gritts, who was standing just inside the door, smoking a cigar and talking with the sheriff.

For a moment, everyone froze. Clint recovered from his surprise first and said, "Everybody relax. This is a friendly visit."

Gritts blew smoke into Underwood's face, and his bloodshot eyes challenged the young man from Chicago. To Clint's way of thinking, Underwood had no chance at all in a fight, either with fists, knives, or certainly guns.

"Let it be," Clint warned as the two big men glared at each other.

"Who's the little trooper?" Gritts asked with a sneer. "Looks like he stepped off the damn chorus line, he's so soft and pretty."

Underwood's fists balled at his sides, and Clint knew he had to get the young Easterner out of the sheriff's office before the man's temper got the better of his senses.

"Damnit!" Underwood protested as Clint ushered him back out the door. "Let go of me!"

"You wait right here," Clint said. "You'll only get yourself a beating at best or killed at worst if you take on Gritts."

"Then that's him!"

"Yes. Now will you just do as I ask for once?"

Underwood managed to nod, but it obviously took him some doing.

Clint eased the gun that rested in his holster, though he doubted that even the pair of vipers inside would try to gun him down in the city sheriff's office.

When Clint returned inside, the two men were on their feet.

"What do you want?" Sheriff Williamson demanded.

"That man who was with me is Andrew Underwood. He just arrived from Chicago."

"So?"

"He's the brother of the dead outlaw I shot during the bank holdup. Underwood wants his brother's horse, saddle, rifle, pistol, and whatever else of value was on his body."

The sheriff swore. "Can he prove he's the outlaw's brother? I won't release a damn thing if he can't."

"He can prove it," Clint said. "I've got the letter that was on the outlaw's body, and he's got identification. Now, do you want me to get the judge, or can we do this the easy way?"

The sheriff knew he was beaten. "All right. All right!" he growled. "But the man didn't have a cent on him when he got to the undertaker's office."

"I can check on that. What about a sidearm and pocket watch? I know he had gun, and I seem to remember a Winchester rifle."

Williamson was fit to be tied, and if it had not been for Gritts's ominous presence looming in the background, Clint could have enjoyed the lawman's exasperation.

"All right, damnit!" Williamson swore. "Here's the outlaw's gun, but I don't know where the hell his Winchester went. If he had one in his saddle boot, it disappeared."

Clint knew that he had no way to enforce an accounting. "What about his pocket watch? I saw it."

The sheriff yanked open the middle drawer of his desk, made a big show of rummaging around, and then slung the watch across his desk. Clint caught it before it struck the floor.

"Good thing you didn't break the crystal," he said, "because if you had, I'd've seen that you paid to have it replaced."

Gritts shifted on his feet. "I reckon the sheriff could afford that, seeing as how him and me hooked up together to capture one of the Blackstone Gang."

"What!"

Gritts beamed. "I guess you heard me. The sheriff here, he got a tip and we followed up on it last night. Trapped one of the murderers, but a couple of others got away. We'll catch 'em, though."

"Let me talk to him," Clint demanded.

"Can't," Sheriff Williamson said. "The man is dead."

"Then I want to see him."

"Sure," Gritts said, "everyone else in town has seen him. Course, seeing as how the Blackstone Gang all wear masks during their holdups except for Blackstone himself, it won't do you much good."

All of a sudden, it struck Clint what was going on. The sheriff and Big Joe Gritts had decided to team up, and since they didn't have a clue as to the real gang members' identities, they were going to kill innocent men and claim the two-thousand-dollar rewards. It was slick, because the entire territory was so desperate to see the Blackstone Gang brought to justice that nobody was going to make a fuss out of Williamson and Gritts collecting the reward money.

"So," Clint said as he studied their smiling faces, "you've made yourselves a little arrangement, have you? What happens when you run out of gang members and the *real* Blackstone Gang keeps robbing and killing?"

Gritts made his best attempt at a laugh, and it was obscene. "I reckon new gang members will get added right along as the old ones get killed," he said. "Seems to me that it ought to work that way."

"And if someone actually kills or captures Harry Blackstone, you'll be out of a very lucrative reward-collecting business, won't you," Clint said.

"We'll worry about that if and when it happens," the sheriff said, looking like the cat that swallowed the canary. "To my way of thinking, that might be years away—if ever."

Clint struggled to contain his anger. This pair had signed on for a campaign of legalized murder that was going to make them halfways rich.

"Tell you what," Clint said, "when I do catch up with the real Harry Blackstone, I'll take him alive. And when he tells a jury about how none of his gang were actually killed by you two, then I think you'll be joining him on the gallows."

Gritts and the sheriff hadn't considered that possibility, and it showed in their shocked expressions. Gritts recovered first and said, "I guess that we won't worry about that too much. Seems to me, a man like you is pretty damn likely to stop a bullet before much longer. I mean, you aren't stickin' much to your little shop down the street, and that Miss Butler tells me that you aren't sleepin' in her bed these days, though I can't figure why not."

"Watch it!" Clint warned, his hand slipping down to his gun butt. "I don't care what the law would call it, but I'll gun both of you down before I'll stand and listen to threats and insults."

"Better back off, Joe," the sheriff said nervously.

Gritts, however, was not of the same mind. "The two of us can take him. What do you say?"

"Hell no!" Williamson cried. "He'll take me out first, and what good will it do me then if you manage to get a bullet through him!"

"Sheriff," Clint said, "I'm glad to see that you're still thinking clearly, because that is exactly what I'd do."

Gritts could see how things were, so he relaxed and said to Clint, "Reckon you're just upset because we already earned us some bounty money. Too bad you got nothing to show for your ride up to Virginia City except a damn boy to nursemaid."

Clint backed out the door. "It'll come down to a gunfight between us," he promised. "And when it does, I'll drop you both."

He turned around and grabbed Underwood's arm, then shoved the pocket watch into his hand. "Recognize this?"

"Yeah. My father gave it to William when he left the last time."

"It's yours now. Along with a damn good roan horse and this six-gun and holster."

"Thank you," Underwood said, "and from what I couldn't help overhearing inside, I guess I'd better take you up on a hide-out gun right now. Maybe I won't have time to become quick on the draw the way those two are acting."

"Good thinking."

They trooped down the boardwalk to the gunsmith shop and Clint unlocked it. It was a small shop, not more than three hundred square feet, but it had plenty of good workspace and benches, which Clint had filled with files and the tools of his trade. He had two good vices and quite a few used holsters that he was selling cheaply.

"Here," Clint said, "let me have a good look at your brother's pistol."

Underwood gave it to him and he inspected it carefully, spinning the cylinder, testing the trigger pull, checking out the balance and the general condition of the weapon.

"Well?"

"It's a damn fine Colt," Clint said, "but the holster and cartridge belt leave something to be desired."

He took down a worn but very serviceable holster and belt, jerked the cartridges out of the old one, and reinserted them in the one he was giving to Underwood. "Strap it on."

Underwood did as he was told. "What do you think?"

"It'll do."

"What was wrong with my brother's holster and gunbelt?"

"The leather was too soft. Slows down the pull."

"Oh."

Underwood strutted around in a tight circle and he smiled. "Feels real good on my hip. Almost like it was always meant to be there."

"It wasn't," Clint snapped.

Underwood's expression grew serious. "Say, those two really got under your skin when they mentioned that Miss Butler, didn't they?"

"I don't want to talk about it," Clint said as he opened another drawer and studied a collection of derringers.

"Well who is she, your sweetheart?"

Clint said nothing as he pulled out a little two-shot, .45 caliber derringer. As he was checking its action, the door to his shop opened and Clint heard Underwood suck in his breath as the young man smiled at Lucinda Butler.

"My Lord!" Underwood breathed. "Would you be . . . would you be Miss Butler?"

"I am," she said, her cheeks coloring slightly as she looked at the tall, young Adonis. "And who are you?"

Underwood bowed, and his eyes never left Lucinda's. "I am Andrew Underwood, late of Chicago but now of Carson City. And I am pleased to make your lovely acquaintance. Mr. Adams and I are going to apprehend the Blackstone Gang together."

Clint snapped the derringer together with a hard CLICK. He didn't like the way that Underwood was looking at Miss Lucinda. He didn't like it one damn bit.

FIFTEEN

Harry Blackstone could feel his control starting to slip as his manhood pistoned rapidly in and out of the beautiful Veronica. He was raised up above her so that he could better study her face and watch the way her eyes began to flutter as she squirmed and undulated under his long, hard body.

He could feel her fingernails biting into his buttocks and he knew that her heels were raking his sheets. Her fine breasts were swollen with desire and her lips were pulled back from her teeth.

"You love this, don't you?" he choked.

"Yes, please, hurry!"

Blackstone was in no hurry at all. He had been working up his desire for nearly twenty minutes, and his entire body ached with a sweet tingling that went all the way down to his toes. His own sensations were heightened immensely by the vision of this half-breed wildcat who was also ready to explode.

Blackstone closed his eyes for a moment and he could feel her milking his manhood, and then he heard her cry out with pleasure and felt her body begin to buck as she lost control.

He was ready as well. "Now," he rasped as he reached down, cupped her muscular buttocks in his hands, and drove himself deep into her body, filling her with his seed as she moaned with satisfaction.

When he rolled off her, Blackstone was grinning wolfishly. "You're as good as I've ever had," he said.

She sat up on his bed and studied him. "Thank you. Would you marry me some day?"

"Hell no."

Veronica blinked, and her eyelids shuttered slightly. "Why not? After all, you've been giving me singing and acting lessons. You said I'd be famous some day. If I am, you had better marry me now and not take any chances of my finding another man."

He snorted. "You're beautiful and you can sing, but I no longer believe you have the talent to become a great actress."

Veronica felt a cold shiver pass through her body. "But you said I reminded you of the great Lola Montez when she was young."

"I said a lot of things," Blackstone snapped with mounting irritation. "But making people believe illusion is my profession. You've got a fine voice, and we can make some money off it and your beauty. But when the beauty is gone, it's over for you and I'll find someone else."

"Someone else?"

"Sure," he said. "That's why I'd never marry a little trollop like you. They get old and wrinkled—women age like spoiled fruit. When they do, you find fresh fruit."

Veronica was on her feet and her eyes flamed. "That's what you think of me? Like fruit!"

"Fresh, beautiful fruit."

"That will spoil!"

Blackstone was running out of patience. "Listen," he said, "you were nothing when I took you off that train. Now I'm going to make you something—what the hell else do you want from me!"

"Your love and your name!" she cried.

Blackstone's patience snapped, and he grabbed the woman

around the throat. Veronica's eyes went wild with fear and she began to struggle as he lifted her to the very tips of her toes.

He was strangling her to death. She gazed into his face and saw not a single hint of mercy, of humanity. Only an animal-like pleasure at her suffering. She tried to knee him in the groin but he twisted his hips, and she felt her strength draining away until he released her to collapse at his feet.

"You're trash," he hissed. "You're just nothing but trash. I'd never give you my name! I'd have to be mad to take you for a wife when I can have you for pleasure as long as I desire and then discard you like dung."

Veronica did not lift her head as his words beat at her. She struggled to regain her breath, feeling her throat ache where his hands had closed on her windpipe. He did not see her face and it was just as well, because at that moment she knew that she was going to bring this man down, even if she had to die trying.

"Get up," he commanded, "and prepare my meal. I've got business to attend to."

Hope flared in Veronica's broken heart. If he were leaving, and if Deke were going with him, then she could escape! And she was sure there must be a great reward for him. After all, he was an outlaw, the leader of a vicious gang.

A hard mask fell across Veronica's beautiful face as she climbed to her feet and stood naked before him. She could feel his eyes boring into her, but she did not meet them.

"I've hurt your feelings again, haven't I?" he asked.

She knew better than to lie. Despite his insanity, he was able to read her mind like a book and had done so many times.

His long, supple fingers traced a line down her throat. "You're going to have some pretty ugly bruises. I'm sorry about that. I lost my temper. But you provoked me, Veronica. You know that, don't you?"

She knew nothing of the sort, but she was smart enough to nod her head.

"Good girl," he said, his hands slipping down to cup her breasts. Then he bent his head and kissed her nipples, nipping and licking them up to a point despite the hatred she felt for him.

He laughed at her. "You're angry at me, but you can't resist my touch. I could make you beg for me if I wanted to, my dear."

"Never," she spat, retreating from him.

His smile died, and she saw a wildness come to his eyes that made her quickly say, "You're right! I would . . . would beg to have you inside of me."

The wildness died, and he smiled. "You try to be so clever. But right now I think you hate me and will betray me at the first opportunity."

"Oh no!"

"Yes you will. And so I will have to tie and gag you while Deke and I are gone."

Veronica shook her head. "Please don't. I promise I'll wait here for you. I . . . I worship you."

But he didn't believe her. "You can prove it again after I return," he said. "But for now, you must submit and do as I say. I promise to be gentle and to return soon. Now, come to me."

Veronica knew better than to argue or resist. Besides, maybe if he was gone long enough, she could untie herself and escape.

When he had finished tying her up, Blackstone descended into the rock basement of his Gold Hill Hotel and carefully applied a darkening grease used by actors to his forehead, cheeks, throat, and hands. Then he used a special paste to attach his black mustache, eyebrows, and spade bit. Finally, he took the black wig from its little rock hiding place.

The entire process of disguise took him nearly an hour, but

he was in no hurry. His men were waiting down in Six Mile Canyon, where he would meet them before they rode north to Reno, where the Washoe Bank was receiving almost $25,000 to be delivered the following day to the Comstock Lode to satisfy mining payrolls.

Blackstone grinned. The cash would reach the Comstock, all right, but the miners would never see it. As usual, he would split the take fifty-fifty and ride away with Deke after agreeing to get together one month later. Blackstone had never shown his real face to anyone in his gang except for Deke. And Deke was so well paid and unimaginative that he would never betray his trust.

Blackstone left his rock basement, and when he stepped outside, it was dark, just as he had planned. Deke was waiting for him, and when they were both mounted, Blackstone reined his horse south.

"I thought we were going to meet the boys in Six Mile Canyon," Deke said.

"We are," Blackstone said, "but I thought we might both pay the Gunsmith a little visit."

Deke was a man who took his orders and kept his mouth shut, but this time he could not hold his silence. "Mr. Blackstone, that Gunsmith is one man you should just leave be. He's big trouble."

"I mean to kill him," Blackstone said. "And I will. I'll keep trying until I catch him in my gun sights."

"But Mr. Blackstone, you're a rich man now. Why don't you just hire somebody to ambush him!"

"Hire somebody? Like who?"

"Any of the gang would do it for the right price."

Blackstone's morbid curiosity was piqued. "And what would be the 'right price'?"

"A thousand dollars," Deke said quickly, his mind quite certain that that sum would entice anyone.

"Would *you* take the job for that amount of money?"

"Why, I sure would!"

Blackstone reined in his horse. "All right then," he said, turning the animal about. "In that case, we will go directly to Six Mile Canyon just as planned. But after we rob the Washoe Bank tomorrow, I want you to ride to Carson City and wait until you have the opportunity to kill the Gunsmith."

"For a thousand dollars, I'd kill a dozen Gunsmiths," Deke said. "But there is one thing I'd like thrown in on the deal."

"What?"

"Veronica," Deke said nervously. "Just lookin' at her has driven me near crazy. I've been using up whores faster than I can tell you, and I'm still crazy for that half-breed woman of yours. And I know you're humpin' some other women up in Virginia City. So if you don't mind, just havin' her once or twice is what I really want."

Blackstone chuckled. "She's really gotten to you, hasn't she?"

"She's all I think about day and night," Deke confessed. "I never wanted any woman the way I want that one. But I'd never take her without your permission. I swear I wouldn't."

"I know that," Blackstone said, "and if you kill the Gunsmith, I'll let you have her for a night, along with the thousand dollars. How's that for being fair?"

Deke felt his manhood start to enlarge and fill his pants. "It's mighty damn fair," he breathed, "and as soon as we get the bank robbed, I'll be on my way to Carson City."

"Good," Blackstone said, privately deciding that it was about time he eliminated both Deke and Veronica. Maybe he'd let the ugly little man satisfy himself first, but then it would be time to just kill them, sell his hotel, destroy his disguise, and move up to Virginia City.

Yes, he thought, it was time for Harry Blackstone, the most wanted and hated outlaw in Nevada, to simply vanish forever.

One more job would give him enough money to buy Piper's Opera House and refurbish it to an elegance sufficient to attract the greatest of American and European thespians.

And he would find himself another little trollop to seduce with dreams of fame. Admittedly, it would be difficult to find one as beautiful as Veronica, but if a man had money and influence, as he would have when he owned Piper's Opera House, he could always find beautiful women to seduce.

Always.

SIXTEEN

The gang was waiting at the head of Six Mile Canyon just as Blackstone had ordered, except that two members were missing.

"Where's Charlie and Ed?" Blackstone demanded.

"They bought a couple of bullets about a week ago over in Reno," one of the outlaws said. "I guess they tried to pull off a job on their own."

Blackstone swore in anger. "Goddamnit! I thought I'd made it plain—nobody works on their own! You ride under my orders or you don't ride at all. Now look what happened! There's only five of us instead of seven!"

"Five ought to be enough for the job," Deke said quietly. "We'll each have a bigger split."

Blackstone saw it differently. Since he was getting half of the loot anyway, it didn't help him at all to have too few guns. For a moment, he almost decided to hell with it—he would call the job off. Five men was cutting things pretty thin.

"I don't know," Blackstone said, pulling his drooping Stetson down low over his face as a rider galloped past. "I'd counted on seven of us, and now there are only five. I'm going to have to think about this awhile."

"Well, why don't we make camp over in those trees and think about it," one of the outlaws suggested. "Or better yet, go on into Reno and get a hotel, a bottle, and a few women."

"No," Blackstone snapped, "we'll make camp just as we planned and I'll give you my decision in the morning."

Deke and the other outlaws exchanged glances, and Deke said, "I guess we'd better do as Mr. Blackstone told us, huh, boys?"

The three men nodded. They had made a pile of money riding under Harry Blackstone but they all agreed he was half crazy.

That night, they made a small campfire and turned in early. To any passerby, they looked like dozens of other little collections of men that passed daily on their way to and from the Comstock Lode. Maybe better mounted and dressed than most and certainly standoffish, but still they raised no suspicions.

The next morning, hours before sunrise, Blackstone woke them all in the cold darkness and said, "We'll break into the bank before daylight and be waiting for the manager to open it."

"With that much money in his bank, there's liable to be a couple of guards with him when he comes to open for business."

"If we're inside waiting, they'll be caught by surprise. We let them come in, and then we get the drop on them as they're guarding the front door. It'll be easy enough. Then we leave before the town even wakes up to the fact that their bank has been robbed. We've never done anything like that before, and we'll catch them with their pants down around their ankles."

The outlaws nodded and, still half asleep, they grumbled as they rolled out of their blankets and silently began to get dressed and saddle their horses.

"Shore wish we had time for a cup of coffee," one of the gang members complained. "I ain't got up this early since I worked for a livin'."

"Me neither," another one said, "but if we get to split twelve thousand among the four of us, that's three thousand each. I can buy a freight car of whiskey for that much cash."

"I always dreamed of fillin' a bathtub with French champagne and fucking in it till the bubbles all went flat," another man said.

"Let's saddle up!" Blackstone ordered in the darkness. "I mean to be inside that bank before daylight."

They were in the saddle moments later and riding abreast through the sage toward Reno. The stars were dying out, and somewhere off in the hills a pair of coyotes were mourning the passing of another hungry night.

"You got any idea how we're going to break into a bank?" Deke asked his boss.

"I sure do," Blackstone said. "I told you I checked it out about a month ago and I had a man watching for this payroll. There have been arrangements made for us."

Deke was not at all sure what "arrangements" meant, but even though the man he rode for was crazy, he was crazy like a fox, and Deke had full confidence that they could successfully rob the Washoe Bank and make a clean getaway.

"Mr. Blackstone, you sure don't miss a thing, do you?"

"Not if I can help it. But I'm counting on you to hold up your end and help make sure the others do the same."

"I will," Deke promised, "same as I always have. And when we get out of here, I'm headin' straight for Carson City. I mean to kill the Gunsmith and have a taste of that half-breed girl, like you promised."

"Sure thing," Blackstone said. "I'm a man of my word."

When they rode into Reno, it was about an hour before sunrise and the last of the stars were gone. Blackstone had his riders dismount and tie their horses in the alley a half block south of the Washoe Bank, and then he disappeared for nearly twenty minutes. When he returned, he had a key and a smile on his face.

Holding the key aloft, he said, "This ought to do it."

"How'd you get that!"

Blackstone chuckled. "The banker managing this establishment has been seeing a certain 'lady' of the evening, even though he is supposed to be a pillar of his community. One night he must have dropped this key on the way out the woman's window. Pity, huh?"

The gang members grinned. One said, "I'll bet that key didn't come cheap."

"No," Blackstone admitted, "it came very dear. It cost me a considerable amount of my share of the money, but that is not of your concern. Now, let's go inside and prepare a welcoming committee before it gets light enough for anyone to see us."

Ten minutes later, they were inside the bank. Blackstone made sure that all the curtains were tightly drawn over the windows, and then he lit a lantern and had a try at the huge vault.

"Any luck?" Deke asked.

"No," Blackstone said. "I'm afraid I'm no safecracker. We'll just have to wait until the manager arrives and then have him open this damn thing."

They all looked up at the clock on the wall. It was just seven-thirty. They had a two-and-a-half-hour wait.

"Wake me at nine o'clock," Blackstone said. "That's when the manager and his head clerk arrive to open the bank and get things in order."

"What about the guard?"

"There will be one along when this place opens for business," Blackstone said as he neatly folded his coat up for use as a pillow before he hopped up on the counter and prepared to take a short nap. "But he's an old man. Wears a handlebar mustache and looks like an old-time marshal."

"He just might be dangerous," Deke said.

"Then use your knife and cut his skinny old throat," Blackstone said as he closed his eyes and drifted off to sleep.

Deke and the others were much too nervous to have napped even if their leader had allowed such a thing. They each prowled around and around inside the bank, rifled the manager's desk, and found his cigars and smoked them while they waited.

And then, exactly at nine o'clock, just as Blackstone had predicted, they saw two men approaching the bank, accompanied by an old man wearing two pearl-handled guns on his skinny hips.

"It's the guard," Deke said, waking up his boss. "They're coming with the guard!"

Blackstone was awake instantly, and he dashed to the window, pulled the curtain aside an inch, and peered out at the three men who were approaching. Blackstone had already familiarized himself with all three, but the guard did not normally come in until the bank was open for customers.

"He's here early because of all the cash in the vault," Blackstone said. "Deke, take care of him. No gunshots, no cries for help. Understand?"

Deke nodded. He was not sure, but he thought his boss expected him to cut the old guard's throat. Well, that wasn't his style, so he'd just crease the old fart's skull with the barrel of his Colt and that would do quite nicely.

"All right, everybody get down where you won't be seen. As soon as the three of them are inside, I want that door shut behind them. We'll be in and out of that vault in ten minutes if there are no hitches."

Deke squatted behind the front door and drew his gun. He listened as the key was turned in the lock. He could hear their voices but not clearly enough to understand the words. The three sounded to be in good spirits. No wonder: *They* hadn't been awakened four hours before daylight.

When the door opened, they marched inside talking, and Deke saw the old man really was wearing two guns, and they looked well oiled and well used.

Deke came to his feet, but his crouch had cut off the circulation in his right leg, and he came upright off-kilter enough to require grabbing the door for support.

The sound Deke made wasn't much, but the old guard had heard it, and spun around with amazing quickness for a geezer his age. The man had pale blue eyes and pale blue veins ridging his forehead. Deke lunged at him with his pistol, but damned if the old man didn't whip those two old Colts out of his twin holsters and open fire.

Deke was on him at about the same instant that the pistols went off. His pistol crashed down against the guard's head, sending him to the floor, but not before a bullet had slammed into Deke's shoulder, twisting him down and sending his gun skidding across the lobby.

With the gunfire, all hell broke loose. The bank door was hanging wide open, and everyone in Reno could hear the firing.

Deke looked up to see Blackstone raise his gun and shoot both the manager and the clerk, killing the manager where he stood and wounding the clerk.

"Let's get out of here!" Blackstone yelled.

Deke pushed himself to his knees and then climbed to his feet. "Mr. Blackstone," he cried, "help me to my horse!"

"Sorry," Blackstone said, "but for you, this is the closing curtain."

Deke grabbed for his boss as the man shot him in the face, then jumped for the door. Blackstone's slug ate through Deke's right cheek, furrowed his tongue, and then blew a hole out through the left cheek.

Deke howled with pain and spat blood as Blackstone and the rest of the gang bolted over him with guns blazing as they raced for the alley and their waiting horses.

"Come back, damn you!" Deke screamed as he choked and spat. "Come back!"

Deke pulled himself to the doorway and slammed it shut, then threw the bolt that the manager must have used to keep out anyone while he was inside alone before business hours.

He could hear the sound of heavy gunfire out in the street, and Deke pulled himself over to the window and tore the curtain aside just as Blackstone and just one badly wounded member of his gang swept by in a hail of bullets.

"Get that crazy sonofabitch!" Deke spat and swore in a bitter frenzy. "Kill him!"

But as luck would have it, Blackstone made it through the swirling gunfire. Deke tore his handkerchief from his pocket and shoved it into his mouth to soak up the blood. If he didn't bleed to death in the next few minutes, he knew that he was as good as dead anyway. The townspeople would never allow him to get out of this building alive.

"Help me," the wounded bank clerk groaned. "Please help me!"

"Help your damn self!" Deke cried, his voice muffled and torn.

SEVENTEEN

It was a nice morning as Clint stood beside the Carson River with Andrew Underwood and said, "Now, when your hand moves down to pull up that Colt on your hip, don't be in too much of a hurry. The most important thing in learning the draw is to master the fundamentals. You do that by building up to speed, not trying for it all at once."

Underwood nodded. He planted his feet wide apart and, just as Clint had been telling him all morning, he concentrated on making a smooth drawing motion rather than a hurried, jerky one.

"Now!"

Underwood's hand swept down, hit the butt of his gun, and brought it up as he thumbed back the hammer. Then he shoved the Colt out a little and fired at the big cottonwood tree.

"Damn! Missed it again!"

Clint smiled. "But not by more than, oh, ten or fifteen yards, I'd guess."

Underwood's cheeks colored with embarrassment until Clint added, "Actually, you were pretty darn close. Just slow the motion down a little, and when the gun comes up, point it like you would your index finger."

"That's what I keep trying to do," Underwood complained. "But I don't know, it doesn't seem to work."

"Watch," Clint said, and his hand flashed down to the gun on his hip and the Colt seemed to appear as if by magic in his fist. The weapon barked twice, and pieces of bark splintered from the tree and landed in the river.

"Wow!" Underwood exclaimed. "You think I'll ever be that good?"

"I don't know. I've been practicing all of my adult life. Had to in order to stay alive. Once you get a reputation, the gunfighters start coming."

"Is that why you officially retired?"

"That's right," Clint said.

"Only now," Underwood reminded, "you've got Big Joe Gritts and the sheriff out to nail your hide to a barn door."

"Any way they can," Clint said, his expression growing dark and troubled. "You can see that they plan to kill innocent people and claim the reward money. I know that and so do you. That means we're a threat to what could become a mighty profitable scheme."

"Then I better keep practicing," Underwood said, "or I won't stand any chance at all against them."

Clint didn't think it worth telling the younger man that he could practice night and day for a year and still not stand a chance against Big Joe Gritts. The man was just too experienced and fast.

"Somebody is coming in a real big hurry," Clint said, seeing a rider appear and hearing his name being called.

Underwood forgot about practicing the fast draw. "Trouble?"

"I'd guess it wasn't any social call," Clint said, heading out to meet the horseman.

"Mr. Adams! The Blackstone Gang was shot down this morning trying to rob the Washoe Bank in Reno!"

The rider jumped off his horse, his face alive with excitement. "Mr. Adams, they need you!"

"Why?"

"Because Blackstone is the only man that got away, but one of his gang members is trapped in the bank. He's threatening to kill some people inside unless he can speak to you!"

Clint and Underwood exchanged questioning glances before Clint turned back to the messenger. "But why?"

"I don't know. He just says he'll kill everybody left alive in the bank unless you come quick. He says he'd rather die in a gunfight anyway than swing from a rope."

"Then let's ride," Clint said, and he swung into the saddle and spurred Duke north, with Andrew Underwood right behind him on the fine roan gelding.

It was early afternoon when they arrived at the Washoe Bank and saw all the commotion. Clint and Underwood pushed their way through the crowd, and when Clint saw a man with a badge, he went straight to him.

"I'm Clint Adams. The one the bank robber has been asking to meet."

The lawman was a deputy, and he immediately rushed Clint over to the sheriff, who said, "That man inside wants to see you. But he says you can't be packing a gun."

Clint unholstered his Colt and handed it to Underwood. "Take care of this."

"Aren't you a little nervous about going in there with a man that has nothing to lose?" Underwood asked.

"Nervous? Nope. I'm downright terrified," Clint said. "And if I get myself killed, then I trust you'll sort of watch out for Miss Butler."

"I sure will!"

Clint did not appreciate the man's enthusiasm as he turned back to the pair of Reno lawmen. "If I don't come out in fifteen minutes, that means I'm dead and you'd better storm that bank."

The men nodded grimly as Clint raised his hands and

marched forward. "Hey, mister," he called. "I'm Clint Adams. You wanted to talk to me?"

Deke sat with his back propped up against the door. He had lost a hell of a lot of blood, and he was so weak he did not think he could stand. The old guard who'd caused all of the trouble was awake too and glaring at him through a mask of dried blood from the pistol-whipping he'd taken. They'd talked some, and Deke had discovered the old feller had been a Texas Ranger and was tougher than boot leather.

"He's here," the old man hissed.

"I hear, the same as you." Deke scooted out of the way of the door and then he managed to slide the bolt free and edge himself around so that he could keep both the old Ranger covered as well as the Gunsmith when he entered the bank.

"You armed?" Deke choked, his voice sounding strange and his tongue feeling like a burning rag in his mouth.

"No!"

"Then come inside with your hands up!" Deke shouted. "One false move and I'll kill innocent people in here."

Clint opened the door and stepped inside. The first thing he saw was the old man with dried blood on his face. Next he saw the dead bank manager and then the young clerk, who was moaning with his head cradled in his hands.

"You all right, boy?"

"He'll live if you don't try any tricks," Deke said, cocking back the hammer of his Colt.

Clint turned to study the outlaw who had a gun trained on him. For a long minute they measured each other, and then Deke said, "You don't look so damned special to me, Gunsmith."

"I'm not special at all."

"Except for the fact that you've put a hell of a lot of fast men in the grave."

Clint didn't deny the fact, but neither did he acknowledge

it. It was easy to see that the outlaw had lost a lot of blood and was almost ready to collapse. The gun in his fist was unsteady, and his face was gray with pain. "What do you want of me?" asked Clint.

"I want you to kill Harry Blackstone. The sonofabitch left me here to die!"

Clint was astonished. Before he could form an answer, the outlaw said, "Old man, you take that boy and get him out of here right now, while I'm feeling generous."

But the ex-Ranger hesitated. His pale, flinty eyes darted from Clint to the gun in Deke's fist. "You gonna kill him in cold blood?" he asked. "Is this some kind of a trick to get him alone and kill him slow, Apache style?"

Deke cackled a laugh. "You suspicious old sonofabitch! I'm half dead, you look *worse* than death, and the kid is going to *be* dead if he don't get to a doctor. Now get him the hell out of here before I change my mind and shoot you both!"

"Better do as he says," Clint said.

The old man nodded and pushed to his feet. He was speaking to Clint when he said, "You probably don't remember me. I was before your time, but I saw you once in Abilene when you stood up to the Anton brothers and gunned all three down in a fair fight. I sure would hate it if that ugly little bastard over there with the gun isn't telling the truth and—"

Deke put a slug between the old man's boots. "Next one takes off your shriveled, useless old balls," he warned.

The ex-Ranger bristled. "Not so damned useless yet!"

"Get out of here!"

The old man reluctantly grabbed the young clerk and dragged him out the doorway.

"Sit down," Deke said. "Just keep your hands away from your sides and listen."

Clint did as he was told.

"Blackstone wears a disguise," Deke said, wanting revenge before he cashed in his own chips in his own fashion. "He wears a black wig, beard, and eyebrows, and he lives in the Gold Hill Hotel."

"Where does he keep all the money he's stolen?"

"I don't know. Maybe in the rock basement. He never let me or Veronica down there."

"Who is she?"

"That half-breed woman we took off the train. She's all I could think about for a long time now. Dyin' without having her first is a hard thing to face."

"What is Blackstone's *real* name?"

"I never knew. Maybe John Piper does. Blackstone is his friend and acts on his stage. But none of that matters now, does it?"

Clint studied the man closely. "No," he said, "which brings us to you and me."

"Yeah. Do you think you can get me a prison sentence?"

"You just had the decency to let two innocent men go free," Clint said. "And if you aren't planning to kill me so that I can capture Blackstone, then I'll gladly speak to a judge on your behalf."

"Uh-uh," Deke said, "you don't quite get it. You see, I want Blackstone *dead*, not captured. He has to be tortured and then killed, you savvy?"

"I won't do that."

Deke sighed. He raised his gun and pointed it at Clint's heart. "You got two choices right this minute. Either give me your word that you'll kill him and do it slow, or I'll pull this trigger."

Clint swallowed. This man wasn't bluffing. He had nothing to lose. "All right," he said, knowing full well that he would take Blackstone alive if he could and that the man would suffer most by waiting to hang. "You win."

Deke chuckled and then began to cough. Flecks of blood blew out of his cheeks and Clint looked away.

"Maybe some water is what you need," Clint said.

"Yeah. Get . . . get me some water!"

Clint hurried for the open door, half expecting to hear a shot and feel a bullet rip through his heart. And when he did hear the shot, his heart almost stopped in his throat.

But he was alive. Shaken, he turned and looked back over his shoulder and saw the outlaw staring up at the ceiling with a fresh gunshot hole leaking from his temple.

EIGHTEEN

As soon as Clint was sure that nothing more could be gained at the Washoe Bank, he pushed aside all the questions and managed to reach Underwood.

"Let's ride," he said in a terse voice.

"But what—"

"Later!" Clint snapped as he stepped into the saddle, avoiding the questions of the sheriff and a newspaper reporter from the *Reno Evening Gazette* who was hounding him unmercifully for a story.

Clint touched spurs to Duke's flanks and sent the black gelding forward so that the crowd had little choice but to make way or risk being trampled. They rode down Virginia Street and then angled up toward the Comstock Lode.

When they had ridden several miles at a hard gallop and reached the Virginia City turnoff, Clint finally reined his horse in for a breather before they tackled the steep uphill climb to the Comstock Lode.

Underwood was none too pleased by the brusque way Clint had earlier shunted aside his questions, and he made his feelings known. "What the devil is wrong!" he demanded. "I've got a right to know where we're heading and for what reason."

"I'd like you to go on to Carson City," he said. "I've got some business to take care of in Gold Hill."

"Oh no you don't!" Underwood cried. "You know something and you're not telling me."

"It's better that I do what I have to do alone," Clint said.

But Underwood wasn't buying that. "Is it the damned reward money? Is that why you're trying to get rid of me? So you can claim it all by yourself?"

Clint felt insulted and started to ride past, but Underwood reached out and grabbed his reins. "Wait a minute. I want you to know I don't want any of the money. I just want to help see that Blackstone pays for my brother's death! Can't you understand that?"

"Yeah," Clint sighed, "I guess I can at that."

Underwood released his reins. "So where is he?"

"At the Gold Hill Hotel. He's been wearing a disguise, and that's why no one has been able to identify him. He's an actor."

"Then Mr. Piper lied to us that day."

"I doubt it," Clint said. "Most likely Blackstone used an alias. There is no reason to suspect that a man like Piper would have anything to do with a vicious killer."

"So what is your plan?"

Clint looked up at Sun Mountain. "Blackstone has a hostage—a half-breed girl named Veronica that was kidnaped from the V. and T. Railroad. I'd say that she is our first concern. We need to get her safely out of that hotel before the lead starts flying. And besides Blackstone, there's a lot of stolen money to be found."

Underwood nodded. "You find the girl and the money, I'll take care of Blackstone."

"Not a chance," Clint said. "You couldn't even hit that cottonwood tree, remember? And it wasn't even shooting back at you. Blackstone is a crazed killer. I mean no offense, Andrew, but he is not a man that a greenhorn like you would meet and walk away from."

Underwood's pride was injured, but he had to admit that Clint was probably right. He had been in a few fistfights but never a gunfight, and he had no reason to be confident about his ability to outshoot a real Western outlaw leader.

"All right," he said, "I'll take responsibility for the girl's safety. Maybe she knows where the money is hidden. Either way, you can keep the reward."

"If we recover the money stolen from the Carson City bank, we'll split the reward," Clint said. "Otherwise, we'll divide it up among those who lost their savings."

"You're a real samaritan, aren't you," Underwood said.

Clint chose to ignore the remark as he pushed his horse into a trot and headed up to the Comstock. He just hoped that Blackstone had not already fled with his thousands and thousands of dollars of stolen money.

Blackstone had ripped his disguise away while fleeing Reno. As luck would have it, he came upon a horseman still asleep in the cottonwood trees, and he quietly swapped horses with the man and continued on toward the Comstock Lode, climbing up the steep Six Mile Canyon into Virginia City.

By the time Blackstone crossed over the Divide and started down the other side of the mountain into Gold Hill, he had concluded that he had nothing to fear. He'd personally shot that last surviving member of his gang before they'd ridden a mile, and Deke was also gone.

Now with a fresh horse and his disguise stuffed into his saddlebags, there was only one person still living who knew that he was really Harry Blackstone, head of a now-decimated outlaw band. And that one person was the beautiful half-breed girl who lay gagged and bound in his hotel.

It was, Blackstone thought, a real waste and a pity that beautiful Veronica would have to be eliminated. He was not yet sure how he should do this, but he would try to think of some way to take care of her without a great deal of pain or fuss. Perhaps he would bury her corpse in his basement and then take his money and offer to buy Piper's Opera House the next day. He would not have quite enough money to refurbish it in the lavish style that he had hoped, but, by his own accounting, he would have enough to open it and keep it running a good many years, even at a loss.

When he finally arrived at his hotel, Blackstone tied his horse in the thickets behind the building with the idea of turning the animal free after dark. In that way, there would be no links between himself and the robbery at the Washoe Bank.

He mounted his steps, used a key on his front door, and entered his always vacant hotel.

"Veronica," he called up the stairs toward his bedroom, suddenly feeling almost giddy by his good fortune to be the only man among his gang to escape death in Reno.

"Veronica, I'm back!"

Veronica heard his voice and then the stairs creaking as he mounted them one by one. After working at her bonds all night and all this very morning, she had finally just gotten free and had been debating whether to run or to remain and try to uncover the stolen money.

Now it seemed to her that she had no option but to fight for her life. And with that decision, she grabbed a heavy vase and stepped behind the bedroom door even as his footsteps sounded in the upstairs hallway.

The thought entered her mind that, if she failed to knock him senseless with her very first blow, he would grab her by the throat and kill her with his bare hands.

NINETEEN

The doorknob turned, and the sound of Veronica's heartbeat filled her ears as she raised the vase overhead and held her breath.

"Veronica, my darling," he said as he stepped into the room—and she chopped the vase downward, aiming for the back of his head. "I—"

His instincts were remarkable. A warning had sounded in his brain, and Blackstone twisted to see the vase rushing into his eyes. He cried out and managed to raise his hand, partially deflecting the blow, which still smashed his nose and knocked him to the floor.

Dazed and struggling to defend himself, Blackstone tried to roll away from danger, but Veronica was wild with hatred, and she snatched up a half-filled bottle of whiskey and struck him again, and he lost consciousness.

When Blackstone awoke, he was bound hand and foot, though he could feel by the lack of tension on the ropes that the job was poorly done. What concerned him most was that his nose was quite obviously broken and clotted with blood, so that he could not breathe properly.

"Where is it?" she asked, holding his own gun trained on him. "I've looked in the basement and in your room—where is the money!"

Blackstone pushed aside his fear and said, "You will never

133

find it without my help, and I'll never give it."

She cocked the hammer of his gun back and said, "You *will* help or I'll kill you."

He took a long breath and then shook his head. "I know you too well to take that threat seriously. You're not a killer, Veronica. You haven't the courage to execute me."

"You're wrong!" she cried, the gun shaking in her fist.

"No," he said, "I am, if nothing else, an excellent judge of character. You simply are incapable of executing me, though I have no doubt you would pull that trigger if I made a threatening move."

Veronica wanted to pull the trigger, but he had pegged her true: She couldn't kill a helpless man—even a remorseless killer like the one that lay tied before her.

"I will keep you like this, just as you kept me when you were gone. And I'll find that money, damn you! I'll find it if I have to tear every rock and brick out of this hotel!"

He used his forearm to wipe his face of blood. "Why don't we do this the easy way? You help me and I'll give you a share."

"Uh-uh," she said with a mocking grin. "I loved you and trusted you once, but that's past now. I want *all* the money!"

"Don't be a greedy fool!" he snapped. "A posse is on the way. Deke and my entire gang were killed this morning. There isn't much time left to get the money and escape."

Veronica frowned. She looked to the door. Where *was* Deke? He'd always been close by, and it stood to reason that he would be around immediately after a holdup.

"You killed him," she blurted. "If he's dead, it was you that killed him."

"He was shot in the bank-robbery attempt like all the others," Blackstone said. "We got nothing but bullets. A posse is on my trail this very minute, and if they find me, you won't get a cent of the reward money or the fortune I have hidden in this hotel."

He smiled, his confidence growing. "It's all or nothing, Veronica. You can leave rich or with little else but the clothes you wear—just like when I found you. What's it to be?"

He had her. Veronica knew that he had her, and it made her so furious she almost pulled the trigger because she hated this man.

"Easy," he said, sensing that the finger of death was reaching out to touch him, "don't throw everything away!"

"I hate you!" she screamed, swinging the gun at him and wanting to knock that superior look from his face.

He ducked back and she missed. He tried to trip her, but she fell away from him and scrambled to her feet before he could gain some advantage over her. Veronica was so shaken that it took her a moment to gather her scattered wits.

"All right," she whispered, "I'll untie your ankles so you can stand and take me to the money. But I'll never untie your wrists!"

"Very well," he said quite calmly.

Veronica kept the gun trained on him as she edged forward and then quickly untied his ankles.

"Now, get up and take me to it," she ordered.

He came heavily to his feet. With a smile that chilled rather than warmed her, he said, "Follow me."

"One false move and I'll shoot you in the back."

"I'm aware of that," he said as he raised his chin and moved through the door, out into the hall, and then down the steps all the way to the cold, dark basement.

"It's hidden in here."

"I thought so!"

"But to find it," he said, "I'll need you to light a lantern. Unless, of course, you'd rather we explored the room in total darkness."

"No!" Veronica lowered her voice. "No. Where is the lantern?"

"Hanging right here on a nail," he told her, stepping aside.

There was enough light from the stairwell so that Veronica could just see the lantern now. She edged closer, using her gun to motion him back deeper into the darkness. Snatching the lantern up, she placed it down on the cold dirt floor, only to realize she had no matches.

"There are some in my vest pocket," he said, reading the sudden alarm in her face, "but I'm afraid that, with my hands tied, I can't reach them for you."

She saw his game and tried to decide whether or not it would be safer to go back up the stairs to find matches or risk taking them from him.

"You'd better hurry up and decide," he told her quietly. "The posse ought to be here any minute. Pity that would be, with over seventy thousand dollars not ten feet from where I'm standing."

"Show me!"

"I can't. Not in the dark."

She swallowed nervously and moved forward, her eyes fixed on his bound wrists and his vest pockets. Pulling the gun back with her right hand, she reached out as far as possible with her left hand toward his vest.

His right foot swept out and struck her in the side of the knee. The gun in her hand exploded, and Veronica cried out in pain as she fell and he landed on her. The gun was knocked from her grasp and he cursed, then struck her.

Veronica knew that he was going to kill her. She cried out, and her fingernails lanced at his eyes. He swore again and grabbed his face, and she rolled away into the blackness of the basement.

"I'll kill you!" he screamed as she blindly retreated deeper into the darkness, knocking over a barrel, striking a heavy supporting timber, and crabbing her way across a cluttered room.

Veronica's hand swept the floor in a vain search for the missing six-gun as he raged like a man gone insane.

But then suddenly, and for no reason that she could understand, he vanished from the basement doorway and was gone.

Veronica was trembling and certain that he would reappear any moment with a lantern. His hands by now would be untied, and he would then raise the lantern and come to strangle her, and she would be absolutely powerless. Veronica was dead certain her own life was over, and perhaps that was not so bad if she died quickly, because her life had been one terrible disappointment after another. No man had ever wanted her for herself, only for her body. It had been that way almost as long as she could remember, and now . . . now she was about to die, trapped in this basement like an animal.

Forcing herself to act, she began to crawl back toward the rectangle of faint light that marked the doorway. There was a gun on the floor here somewhere. If she could find it before he returned, then she might have a chance. It was a small one, but even that was something.

With her heart pounding, she dropped to her stomach and began to use her entire body to twist and spin around in an attempt to feel as much surface as possible.

She could hear his running footsteps upstairs, and when they again sounded on the stairs, she felt the lost Colt revolver. Sobbing with joy, she grabbed the gun and aimed it at the doorway as he descended the stairs with a glowing lantern.

Veronica waited until he appeared before her in what seemed like a brilliant box of light, and then she pulled the trigger.

TWENTY

Clint heard the gunshot just as he was swinging down from his horse, and he drew his six-gun.

"I hope to God that he hasn't just shot that poor half-breed girl!" Clint yelled as he rushed the front door, with Underwood right behind him.

The door was locked, and even though they both threw their shoulders to it, the heavy oak resisted them.

"The window!" Clint shouted. "I'll kick in the window, and you go around back and make sure he doesn't escape from the rear of the hotel!"

Clint had no trouble smashing in the window with the heel of his riding boot, but it took him several precious moments before he could squeeze his way inside.

The interior of the hotel was dim, the lobby furniture was dust covered, and as Clint straightened up, he saw a figure on the stairwell. "Freeze!" he yelled.

The man had a gun in one fist and a lantern in the other. He fired from the hip, and his bullet cracked past Clint's ear, sending him sideways behind a couch.

Clint popped up and fired again. He heard a scream as the lantern exploded into flames and came tumbling down the stairs, igniting the old carpet.

Clint jumped up and lunged at the stairwell. When he reached it, the flames were already devouring the kerosene-soaked stairway carpeting, making it impossible to go after his man.

"Blackstone!" Clint shouted. "It's Clint Adams, and I know it's you up there! You've got to jump from the window to save yourself. Throw down your weapon and save your life!"

In answer, the man opened fire down the stairway, his bullets splintering the staircase.

Clint tore off his coat and tried to beat out the flames, but the whipping air only fed the growing inferno.

"Blackstone, where's the girl!"

"She'll roast with me in hell!"

Clint stood in helpless frustration. He could see the flames rushing up the stairs. He knew that Blackstone and the girl had only one chance to survive—and that was by leaping from an upstairs window—but Blackstone, like his betrayed gang member trapped in the Washoe Bank, had nothing to live for except a hangman's rope.

The sweat was pouring from Clint's body as the temperature soared, and the smoke was becoming thick and choking. "Let her go!" Clint raged.

In answer, all he heard was two more gunshots. Clint's shoulders drooped with defeat. A man who was so cold-blooded that he would slit another's throat would have no mercy on a hostage. More than likely, those two shots meant that Harry Blackstone had just shot the poor half-breed girl, then turned the gun on himself. Clint pivoted back toward the broken window, choking and fighting for air. He was almost at the door when he heard a cry for help.

Clint froze an instant. The inferno was starting to roar and it was difficult to hear anything, but then he heard another gunshot, and this one sounded as if it had come from the basement!

It took him a minute to find the stairwell leading down to the basement, and he was almost gunned down for his trouble. The girl had opened fire on him, and if she had been any kind of shot at all, he'd have been riddled.

"Don't shoot!" Clint bellowed as he flattened himself against the stairwell and peered around the corner into the inky darkness of the basement. "I've come to help get you out of here before the building collapses in flames!"

A moment later, a dirty, scantily clad girl came stumbling out of the basement, and when she saw him, she threw herself into his arms and began to sob.

"Let's get out of here!"

"But there's money hidden down here! Thousands of dollars of stolen money!" she cried. "We can't just leave it!"

Clint twisted around and looked up toward the head of the stairs. All he could see was an orange glow. He was afraid it might already be too late to escape.

"To hell with the money!" he shouted, grabbing the woman by the wrist and yanking her up the stairs. "What good is money if we're roasted to death!"

His words must have penetrated her terror-filled mind, because Veronica stopped struggling and came rushing after him. At the top of the stairs, however, she shrank back from the blistering heat and the roar of the fire, and he thought she might actually have retreated back down into the temporary safety of the basement if he had not grabbed her and thrown her over his shoulder.

He went stumbling through the heat and the smoke, and it was ten seconds of sheer horror. The flames seared his eyes, and the heat baked his skin and almost ignited both him and the screaming woman like a pair of torches. With no hope of finding the door and getting it open, Clint just lunged forward until he struck a window and then crashed his way through it, he and the young woman spilling outside in a shower of broken glass.

With fresh air pouring through the window, the hotel fire roared like an animal being fed, and Clint grabbed the half-breed woman by a piece of her dress and dragged her skidding across the yard.

Onlookers had already come running, and Clint and Veronica were both lifted to their feet and ushered quickly away from the fire as the clapboard hotel began to buckle and then slowly fold into itself in a shower of fiery embers that lifted far into the sky.

The woman clung to the Gunsmith, sobbing and squeezing his neck as if he were her last hope, which he supposed he had been. People were shouting, and Clint heard the ringing bell of an approaching volunteer fire company. He stared up at the inferno, thinking that, even though the money were lost, at least it was the end of Harry Blackstone.

The girl finally looked up into his face. "Who are you?"

"Just a man who wanted to be the one to see Blackstone's life end."

The girl twisted around and stared at the flames. "I can't believe it's over. That he's dead and the money is gone!"

Clint studied her soot-streaked face. She had been through horrors that he could scarcely imagine, and yet she was still quite beautiful. A good part of her dress had been torn away, so he removed his coat and covered her shoulders before he buttoned it to hide her exposed breasts.

Clint was a little ashamed of himself for staring at her. No wonder Blackstone had taken her hostage and kept her for his pleasure.

"Who will get the reward?"

The question was not the one Clint had expected, and he pushed the young woman back a little. "I . . . I don't know," he said. "I suppose you will."

"It's half yours—I guess—but I'll fight for all of it."

He did not care. "Fine. I think it's small compensation for what you must have been through in the past few weeks."

Before she could reply, several local women were all over them, and they quickly escorted the young woman away.

"Clint!"

The Gunsmith pushed himself to his feet. His own shirt was scorched and tattered, and his eyes were starting to weep from the smoke and the heat. His skin felt seared, and he knew that his eyebrows, hair, and eyelashes were probably singed away.

"Clint, thank God you and the girl made it out!" Underwood exclaimed.

"Just barely."

"He's swearing he saw Blackstone leap to safety from the west side of the hotel and run away."

"What!" Clint forgot about his pains. "Who's saying that!"

"Big Joe Gritts, of course! He's telling everyone that he even took a couple of shots at the man, but he missed."

"Those gunshots were from Blackstone's gun! He kept firing down the stairwell."

Andrew Underwood shrugged. "That isn't what Gritts is telling everyone who will listen. The sheriff up here is already organizing a search party."

Clint swore in anger. "For what! I know that Harry Blackstone fried in that hotel! You were around back. You didn't see anyone jump for safety, did you?"

"No, but I wasn't on the west side," Underwood admitted. "I couldn't be everywhere at the same time. There was a back door, and that's what I had my gun trained on until the fire got so hot."

Clint ran his fingers through singed hair and expelled a deep breath. So, he thought, Gritts was claiming that Blackstone was still alive. And of course, in the coming weeks and months, he would also claim that Blackstone had recruited a new gang. The reward would stand, and both Gritts and Sheriff Williamson of Carson City could keep on killing innocent people and claiming reward money.

"Are you thinking what I'm thinking?" Underwood asked quietly.

"I'm thinking that Gritts and Williamson are going to resurrect the dead and cash in on it in a big way."

"Is there any way to prove that Blackstone died in that burning hotel?"

Clint watched the white-hot fire. "It's hotter in there than a blacksmith's forge," he said quietly. "There may be a few charred bones, but I seriously doubt it."

Just then a big shout went up from the spectators as the entire hotel collapsed inward upon itself, filling up the basement and sending people back in retreat.

"There go the bones," Clint said, "and the stolen money, unless it was buried."

Big Joe Gritts, his own shirt smoking with the evaporation of his sweat, suddenly emerged from the crowd to come sauntering up to them. He studied Clint and chuckled. "You look like a half-roasted Thanksgiving turkey."

Clint went to reach for his gun, but his fingers were burned and the skin had tightened on his flesh, so that he could not have made a fast draw to save his life.

"Go ahead," Gritts challenged. "There are witnesses, and I'll take my chances against you right now."

"Uh-uh," Clint said, curbing his emotions and willing himself to keep his hands away from his gun.

Gritts snickered with derision and turned to Underwood. "What about you, kid? You're wearing a gun. You want a piece of me?"

"No!" Clint shouted, jumping between the two, because he could see that Underwood was about to make a fatal mistake.

"Another time, then," Gritts said. "Too bad that the terrible Harry Blackstone managed to escape death in that pile of smoking firewood, ain't it?"

"You know he didn't," Clint said.

"I don't know anything of the sort! I saw the man jump from the second-floor window and hit the ground running. I sure wished I could have drilled him. Could have used that reward money. But then, I reckon my day will come."

"It sure as hell will," Clint said in a low, hard voice, "and it won't be very damn long. That I can promise you."

Gritts caught the Gunsmith's meaning and he laughed. "Like a roasted turkey," he cackled as he swaggered away.

TWENTY-ONE

Clint found he was too scorched to ride Duke back down to his room in Carson City, so he accepted a buggy ride instead. By the time he arrived in Carson City, he was in serious pain. His face had not blistered, but the hair was all singed away and his complexion was bright red.

"I'm going to give you a can of Doctor Horton's Famous Horse Unguent," Doctor Olms said, pulling the can out of his bag. "It smells mighty bad, but it's the best thing I ever saw for healing up wire cuts and such on horses, and it's bound to speed your recovery."

Clint took the can, spun the lid off, and took a deep whiff. "Whew!" he swore, "that stuff would knock flies out of the air at fifty paces! Doc, isn't there anything that would work better than this?"

"Nope. The other day I burnt my fingers on a skillet handle. I used some of this unguent, and it took the pain away right quick. It seems to have sort of a painkiller in it that makes the skin numb."

"It makes my nose numb just smelling it," Clint complained.

"Use it anyway," the doctor growled. "Miss Lucinda won't be around anyway for a couple of days. She had some business in Sacramento."

Clint was relieved. He knew he looked like a boiled beet, and he was hoping that he'd present a little better appearance by the time Lucinda returned. The vile-smelling unguent was thick and white with the consistency of cold farm butter. He reluctantly scooped some of it out of the can with his fingers and rubbed a little across the back of his hands.

The soothing effect was almost instantaneous. First it felt cool, then it tingled, and finally it sort of went numb.

Observing Clint's expression of surprise and delight, the doctor said, "I told you it was special. Says the ingredients come from the rain forests of South America. Whatever Doctor Horton put into the stuff, it sure does work."

Clint nodded and scooped up two more globs, which he rubbed into his face. "Bless the good horse doctor," he sighed.

Olms rummaged around in his vest pocket until he found his old corncob pipe, which he carried packed and ready to light. He fired it up with a match and studied the Gunsmith carefully. "They say that Blackstone jumped out his second-story window and got away clean."

"It's a lie that Gritts is spreading so he can keep collecting bounties on anonymous 'gang members' that he and the sheriff kill."

"Are you sure?"

"Of course I'm sure! I was the only one who was there."

"Did you see him die?"

"No, but I didn't have to. Blackstone was a crazy man. I'm convinced of that much. He was the kind of man who would have thought his death heroic, rather than just plain stupid."

The doctor nodded. "Sure too damn bad about the money being lost. That news hit the town pretty hard. There are a lot of folks who were just hanging on, hoping that their life savings would be recovered when Blackstone finally got captured or shot. And then to hear it all went up in smoke, well, they're taking it hard."

"Yeah," Clint said, "I'm sure they are. But it couldn't be helped. I pleaded with that crazy bastard to come down or at least throw down his gun and jump from the window. He wouldn't listen. He *wanted* to die."

"Any chance he might have buried the money somewhere outside the hotel?"

"I don't think so. The half-breed girl told me it was hidden in the basement. But unless it was buried under the floor or hidden back in the rock foundation, it's lost."

The doctor brightened. "Well, it makes sense that it might be safely buried. I mean, nobody is going to leave thousands of dollars just lying around wrapped in butcher's paper."

"That might be true." Clint managed a smile. "But it'll take a day or two for those coals to cool down enough to start digging out that basement. Going to be a long, hard, and dirty job and maybe all for nothing."

"It's plenty worth a try," the doctor said, "because if we don't recover the money, Lucinda is going to wind up penniless, and I'm going to be out most of what I've saved."

"Now Doc," Clint said, "I know that you own property all over this town. Saying you're going to be poor if we don't find that stolen money is just not true."

Caught in his own little white lie, the doctor scowled. "Well . . . well, damnit, I'm going to be hit up for money by every charity in town ten times a year! The people around here know I owe them my livelihood, and I won't be living my ease if I'm surrounded by hardship."

There was a knock at Clint's hotel-room door, and he yelled, "Come in!"

It was Underwood. He had a bottle of whiskey and two glasses. When he saw the doctor, he said, "Whoops! I guess I need another glass."

"There's one over there on the washstand," Clint said.

Underwood found it and filled three glasses. He raised his own and said, "To the death of Harry Blackstone!"

"To his death," Olms and Clint repeated.

They drank the toast, and then Underwood surprised them by announcing that he was returning to Gold Hill.

"What for?"

The young Easterner shifted around on his feet. "Well, I sort of wanted to make sure that the poor girl you pulled out of the hotel was all right. She might need some help, you know."

Clint grinned, and the doctor reached into his medical bag and brought out a second can of horse unguent. "If you're lucky and fast-talking enough, maybe you can charm her into letting you apply this."

"Thanks, but I can't stand the smell of the stuff."

"Well damnit," the doctor groused, "it's not for *your* enjoyment, it's for *her* recovery!"

Underwood took the can and nodded. "Be seeing you in a few days," he said as he backed toward the door. "And don't worry: I'll keep practicing with my gun. About the time you're ready to get out of bed, I'll be down and you'll see that I'm a whole lot faster."

"Okay," Clint said. "Thanks for the whiskey, and I'll only ask you one favor."

"What's that?"

"Stay a mile clear of Big Joe Gritts if he crosses your path. He's not someone to fool with. He'll kill you, Andrew. He's fast and ruthless, and he's not a man you want to fight with your fists, a knife, or a gun. Do you understand me?"

"I'd never run from him, but I won't go out of my way to fight him, either. Sorry, Clint, but that's the best I can agree to."

Clint nodded. "Maybe he'll stick around Carson City and try to figure out some way to put me in a pine box before I convince everyone that Harry Blackstone really did die in that hotel fire."

"Maybe I should stay here then," Underwood offered.

"No," Clint said, "go see the girl. She was real upset, as

you'd expect her to be. Now that she's had time to calm down, perhaps she can think of something that would be important."

"Such as?"

"Such as what part of the basement Blackstone might have used to hide the money in."

Underwood nodded. "I'll question her very closely," he promised.

"Yeah," Clint said, "I'm sure you will."

When the door had closed behind Underwood, the doctor said, "I take it that the half-breed girl is quite a looker."

"She's enough to make any man slaver with desire," Clint said, "but she's a real hellcat. Andrew better watch out, or she'll scratch him up one side and down the other. But to tell you the truth, the thing I'm really worried about is Joe Gritts."

"Why?"

"Because if he even thinks that that girl might know where some of Blackstone's stolen money is hidden outside that basement, he'll come after her."

"Doesn't she have someone to protect her?"

"I don't know," Clint said, "but she sure didn't when Blackstone hauled her off that railroad a few weeks ago."

The doctor nodded, and then they drank again, two men momentarily lost in their own gloomy ponderings.

TWENTY-TWO

By the time young Andrew Underwood had returned to Gold Hill, the hour was late. He rode his brother's weary roan gelding back to the glowing bed of coals that marked the remains of the Gold Hill Hotel.

"Looks like a big roasting pit for a goat or something, doesn't it?" one man asked.

"Yeah," Underwood said, thinking there seemed little chance that the stolen money could survive that kind of heat, unless it was pretty well buried. "Anybody know where that girl went?"

"What girl?"

"The one that Blackstone kidnaped off the railroad."

"Oh, her," another man said. "Well, I heard she was taken in by the the ladies of St. Mary's Catholic church, up in Virginia City."

"Oh," said Underwood, "then I suppose she'll be well cared for."

"Yeah, they'll see that she's fed and clothed. She sure was a beauty, that one. Why, I saw her when she and the Gunsmith busted through the front window. It was miracle that neither one of them got cut much. Boy, that is some piece of woman!"

Underwood was thinking the same thing. "Where, exactly, is this St. Mary's church?"

"Well, it's just downslope from the main drag in Virginia

City, about three blocks. You can't miss the big white cross on the steeple."

"Thanks," said Underwood as he threw the reins over his horse's head, remounted, and rode away. "As long as you got the fire, maybe you ought to roast something."

He rode up over the Divide into Virginia City and had no trouble at all in locating the tall white steeple and cross of St. Mary of the Mountains Catholic Church. He debated whether or not to pay a call at this late hour: Since he was carrying the healing unguent that Doctor Olms had specifically asked him to deliver, he decided that he had a legitimate reason to make a late evening call.

But the church was dark and locked up tight when he rode into its yard, and while Underwood was trying to decide what to do, a priest smoking a pipe stepped out of the darkness and asked, "Can I help you, young man? Perhaps you need to find comfort in the spirit of God."

"Well," said Underwood, "I might at that, but what I was really trying to do was find that poor girl who was rescued from the fire in Gold Hill today. I understand the ladies of your church have generously taken her in."

"That is true."

The priest was a tall, slender man in his late forties. He wore wire-rimmed spectacles, a black coat and pants, a white shirt, and the traditional stiff clerical collar.

"I need to see her, Padre."

"I'm afraid she has probably retired for the night," he said. "Come back tomorrow morning and I'll be happy to see that you make her acquaintance."

Underwood frowned. "The thing of it is, I've some burn medicine from the doctor in Carson City. He asked me to deliver it."

"I'll do that for you."

Underwood felt like an idiot as he shook his head. "I

appreciate the offer, but I'd sort of like to do it myself."

The priest considered this for several minutes as he smoked in reflective silence. "All right," he said. "The girl *is* in some considerable pain from the burns she received. But you must promise to be a gentleman, and you will be chaperoned by Sister Anna and Sister Ramona—as well as myself."

"Oh," said Underwood, unable to keep the disappointment from his voice. "Well, I guess it could wait until . . . "

"Come along," the priest said as he started walking. "The convent where she is being taken care of is just attached to the church but on the other side. It's attached to the rectory in which I and my assistant live."

Andrew Underwood was not a religious person; in fact, he felt rather uncomfortable because of all the lecherous fantasies he'd been having about himself and the girl. He'd pictured himself applying the unguent to her skin and then gradually working his way down to where . . .

"What is your name, lad?"

He was jerked out of his thoughts, and it was a good thing it was dark, or the priest might have seen the color rise in his cheeks.

"Andrew Underwood, Padre."

"Well, Andrew, this girl has undergone a terrible, terrible ordeal. And I'm sure that her welfare is of foremost importance to you, as well as it is to the rest of us."

"Oh, yes sir . . . I mean, Padre."

"My name is Father John. You can tie your horse right here at this hitching rail while I make sure that it is all right with the sisters to pay a quick visit to the girl."

"Tell her that the medicine I bring really smells bad, but it works."

The priest almost smiled. "Perhaps it would be better to say nothing about the smell. They will, I'm sure, make that unpleasant discovery in God's own good time."

"Sure," said Underwood, dismounting as the priest went to the door and knocked softly.

A moment later, Underwood turned to see a stocky nun in a long black robe answer. The pair spoke in whispers, and then the nun bowed. When she raised her head to look at Underwood she was not smiling, and he had the distinct feeling that she was annoyed by his late evening intrusion.

"You may come in," the priest said, "but only for a few moments."

Underwood took the unguent from his saddlebags and hurried inside. The convent was very Spartan, clean, and functional. There was a small altar along one wall, a stove and cooking oven with a fireplace along the opposite wall, and a table in between. Two doors led off from the main room, and he was led past another nun, who was praying at the altar.

"Only a minute or two," the priest warned as Underwood blinked in the dimness to see the girl lying in bed, her black hair fanned out across a pillow. She looked to be asleep, but when he padded forward, her eyes popped open and she started with fear.

"Veronica," the nun said, "this man has come with medicine for your skin. It will help ease the pain."

She stared at Underwood so intently he felt as if she were looking right through him, and he stammered, "I . . . I didn't want to wake you up, miss, but Doctor Olms in Carson City used some of this on Mr. Adams—the man who pulled you out of that burning hotel—and it really helped. I thought you might be needing some."

She said nothing for several moments, then smiled a little and said, "You are very kind. My skin feels as if it is on fire. I'm afraid sleep will be impossible tonight."

Underwood was so taken by her smile that all of his reservations evaporated, and he hurried forward, opening the can and spilling the tin lid, but scooping it up and coming to rest beside her bed.

"It smells terrible," he said, taking a little of the unguent on his finger and applying it to her forearm, where even in the bad light he could see a blister.

She caught her breath as the unguent touched the blister, and he saw her bite back a cry of pain. He rubbed the medicine on very gently, and almost at once, she smiled again.

"That is *much* better."

It was as if she had said something very wonderful just for him alone, and for the first time in his life, Andrew Underwood knew that he had fallen in love. With a complete stranger. A girl who had probably lived a life that would turn his own dear Christian mother's hair white. But he could not help that.

"Here," he said, "let me put a little on your cheeks."

"I can do that," she said, but she did not move, so he rubbed it gently into her cheeks and then across her chin. When his fingers brushed her lips, he went cotton-mouthed.

"Mr. Underwood," the priest said, "I think that Miss Valdez can do the rest."

"Is that your name?" he asked. "Veronica Valdez?"

She nodded.

"It's beautiful."

The priest touched him on the shoulder. "Thank you very much for this mission of mercy. Just leave the medicine and come along, please."

"Can I see her in the morning?"

"Why?"

"I . . . I simply must," he blurted.

"She has no money," the priest said, "so if you think she might have some of the outlaw—"

"No, no," he said quickly. "It has nothing to do with money."

Veronica said, "Please, Father."

The priest looked at the girl, then at Underwood. "You are both adults and free to come and go as you wish. But just remember that while you stay here, Veronica, you are in God's house and must act accordingly."

"I will," she vowed.

The priest nodded and turned to Underwood. "Then you may visit her, but there will be the sisters in the other room and this door must always remain open. I do not question your word, Veronica, but a wise steward does not tempt the wolf with a lamb."

Underwood almost said something but then decided that he'd been called a lot worse things than a wolf and maybe, given his earlier fantasies, it was better that the door did remain open, with the nuns in close attendance.

"Tomorrow," he promised.

She reached up and gripped his hand. "I will dream of it."

Underwood shivered as he turned and was escorted by the three religious folk out the door.

TWENTY-THREE

Joe Gritts was seated in the sheriff's chair, and the sheriff was forced to stand in his own office.

"So what are you going to do?" Sheriff Williamson asked. "If Clint Adams keeps telling everyone that Blackstone really died up there in that fire, and if Blackstone doesn't pull a few jobs in the next few weeks, then we're out of the bounty business."

"Damn clever of you to think that all the way through," Gritts said sarcastically.

The sheriff blushed with humiliation. "Don't banter with me, Gritts. I just don't see how we're going to make any more reward money now that Blackstone is dead. And he *is* dead, isn't he?"

"Yeah, he's nothing but ash. I saw him in the upstairs window. He was going to jump, but I shot him through the head."

"But why! Why didn't you let him jump? We could have claimed the reward."

"Because in the first place, any court of law would say that the Gunsmith was more entitled to it than me! And in the second place, at least by him burning to cinders, we've still got a chance to make some bounty money. That's better than no chance at all."

Sheriff Williamson expelled a deep breath. He had come to

realize that Gritts was not only his physical superior but his mental as well. Gritts was just real damn bright.

"All right, all right. So what are we going to do?"

"I'm going to make good and sure that that half-breed girl doesn't really know where Blackstone hid his holdup money."

"You gonna kill her?"

"I don't know. Got some other fish to fry first. Got to shut Adams up sooner or later. And you've got some work ahead too, Sheriff."

Williamson blinked. Up to now, he'd not done a thing— Gritts had been the one who had all the blood on his hands.

"What do you mean?"

"I mean that you're gonna take a page right out of Blackstone's bag of tricks. If he could wear a black wig and beard, I guess you can, too."

"What!"

"You're a little fatter than I'd like, but you're about Blackstone's height. You'll pull a stagecoach robbery and you'll be wearing a disguise."

"Now wait just a damn minute!"

"No, *you* wait a minute," Gritts said, pushing out of the man's chair and coming to his feet. "I done everything so far, and you sure as hell took part of the bounty for those men I killed and said were Blackstone riders. Now you're gonna start earning your keep."

Williamson stared up at the menacing giant. In truth, Gritts scared the shit out of him. He was the most cruel and frightening man the sheriff had ever known, and during his undistinguished career as a lawman he'd seen some real evil men.

"What do you expect me to do?" he said, swallowing loudly and hating himself.

"You're going to be Harry Blackstone and lead your gang in a stage holdup."

"What!"

"You heard me," Gritts snarled. "I've got a couple of men picked out to help. They'll do the dirty work, but you got to be seen in a disguise so you look like Blackstone."

"It won't work."

"It *better* work, Sheriff!"

"When?" Williamson heard himself ask.

"Tomorrow."

"But that's not time enough!"

"The hell it ain't," Gritts said. "You find a wig and a fake beard and it'll work."

"But where can I find such things?"

Gritts was almost out of patience. "Damnit, that's your problem! Find a black dog and some glue—you can figure it out. I'm going to be busy finding a couple of 'Blackstone men' and then planning the holdup."

The sheriff felt sick inside. What he really wanted to do was call this entire mess off before he got his tail in a crack and then had his neck chopped off. Trouble was, he knew he was in far too deep already, and he did not even want to think about what Gritts would do to him if he either refused to go along with this or double-crossed the exconvict.

"Where will we pull the holdup?"

"I'll tell you when it's time. Just have your disguise ready. And make sure that it's good enough so a scared stagecoach driver will swear he was robbed by Harry Blackstone. That's all you have to do; we'll do the rest."

Williamson nodded weakly. "I sure hope you know what the hell you're doing."

"I most always do," Gritts said as he was leaving.

The next morning before sunrise, the sheriff was jolted out of a fitful sleep by the light of a candle and a rough hand on his shoulder. "Wake up, Mr. Blackstone," Gritts growled. "We got some hard riding to do before the sun rises."

Williamson had slept poorly and suffered nightmares that were now about to come true. "Listen," he pleaded, "maybe we ought to reconsider this idea. I've been thinking that if we—"

Gritts's huge fist grabbed the sheriff by his nightshirt, wadded it up beneath his neck, and hauled him flailing out of his bed to drag him across the wooden floor.

"You want to live or die?" Gritts snapped. "It's your decision, but you'll make it right now."

"Live! I want to live!"

"Then let's see that disguise and let's get your ass dressed. We're hitting the early morning stage from the Comstock."

"But that one has three shotgun guards!"

"So I've heard," Gritts said. "That's no problem, and we might even take a good haul to boot."

The sheriff passed his hand shakily across his eyes, but then he got dressed and strapped his cartridge belt and six-gun around his flabby waist.

"Let's see your disguise."

"Now?"

Gritts nodded, and the sheriff brought out a bag with a black wig, beard, and pair of black eyebrows.

"Put the damn stuff on."

Williamson did as he was ordered. Gritts stood back and surveyed him in the candlelight. "It'll do. Let's go."

The sheriff surprised even himself with an angry outburst: "It's a damn good disguise!"

Gritts was already halfway to the door. He turned and said, "It'll do, I told you. Now come on and let's ride."

As they hid behind some rocks and waited for the stagecoach to come rolling down from the Comstock just after sunrise, the sheriff guessed that things would be all right after all. Gritts had found a pair of tough-looking *hombres* who said little but looked plenty capable of doing whatever was required. It occurred to the sheriff that he was probably the only horseman among the four of them who hadn't ridden the outlaw trail and done this sort of thing before.

"What am I supposed to do?" he asked when the stage was seen to appear about a mile to the west.

"Just let Hank and Ernie take the money and hang back just far enough so that the stagecoach driver sees your face so he'll think that you're Blackstone."

"That's all?" Williamson felt a flood of relief.

"That's all," Gritts said. "Me and the boys will do the dirty work."

"You gonna kill the guards?"

"I guess."

"But—"

"Shut up," the one named Hank spat. "You talk way the hell too much, Sheriff."

The way the man said the word *sheriff* made Williamson feel like dog shit, but he swallowed his pride and buttoned his lip to watch as the stage drew nearer.

It had two outriders with Winchesters, and the third guard was seated beside the driver with a shotgun cradled in his arms. The sheriff had watched this particular stage come rumbling into Carson City a hundred times, and he knew that it never carried passengers. Only gold, silver, and sometimes a sack of cash. The take might be as high as twenty thousand. Whether his share was to be half or a quarter, it was still more money than the sheriff had ever earned before.

"Get ready," Gritts said. "I'll take the outrider on the far side. Ernie, you got the other one. Hank, kill the shotgun guard. And no damn misses!"

"Can't you at least give them a chance to throw down their rifles!" Williamson cried.

"No," Gritts said, "because they wouldn't."

The sheriff knew that Gritts was right. He'd seen all three guards before on the streets of Carson City, and they did not look like the kind of men who would gizzard out in a fight. "What about the driver? He's a family man. Got a wife and seven kids."

Gritts actually smiled. "Why, in that case, he's all yours! You just ride out in front of him and raise your gun and point it at his head. He'll haul that team up, thinkin' that he's being robbed by the terrible Harry Blackstone."

"I like that man. You won't kill him, will you?"

Gritts snorted. "Wouldn't it sort of work against our plan if there were no survivors?"

The three men chuckled and Williamson felt like a dolt, knowing he'd asked a very stupid question.

Gritts raised his rifle and took aim, and the other two did the same. Williamson had to look away because it was going to be a turkey shoot.

The three rifles boomed in unison, and when Williamson glanced up, he saw two riderless horses racing ahead and the shotgun guard slumped over the lap of the driver.

"Go get the money, damn you!" Gritts yelled, smacking Williamson's horse across the rump and sending it bounding forward to intercept the coach.

The rest pretty much happened in a daze. The sheriff, flanked by the other two riders—Gritts had stayed hidden in the rocks—cut the stage off. When Williamson raised his gun and pointed it at the driver, the man hauled in his team and cried, "Don't kill me, Mr. Blackstone!"

"Throw down your strongbox!"

The driver did as he was told. His eyes were round with fear as he kept staring at Williamson, even when Hank and Ernie dismounted and shot the lock to pieces, then began hauling out bags of gold and bundles of cash.

"You gonna kill me, Mr. Blackstone?" the driver whispered.

"I got a wife and seven kids. I swear I won't say it was you who did this."

Williamson almost told the man to go ahead and tell everyone that it had been the Blackstone Gang that had pulled off this robbery. But, playing out his role, he said, "You swear to that?"

"Yes sir, Mr. Blackstone! On a whole stack of Bibles, I do!"

"Then drive on!"

"Thank you, sir!"

The driver cracked his whip and his team raced away, leaving Williamson in a cloud of dust as the two men began to stuff the gold and money into their saddlebags.

That finished, they started to remount, and the moment that they were half on, half off the ground, two rifle bullets boomed across the sage. The shots came spaced incredibly fast together, and both Hank and Ernie died trying to swing their right legs over the cantles of their saddles.

They crashed to the dirt road and lay still as Joe Gritts came galloping up and dismounted. Without a word or a glance at the shocked sheriff, Gritts picked both men up as easily as if they were dolls and threw them across their saddles, then tied them down hard and fast.

"Figured now was as good a time as any to do it," Gritts said, more to himself than to the stunned sheriff. "Better take off that damned disguise. But don't throw it away. You might need it again in a few weeks."

Williamson could do no more than nod his head. Looking at Gritts and the work he'd just done as nonchalantly as if he'd shot a couple of bucks in the trees, Sheriff Williamson knew that, sooner or later, Big Joe Gritts figured to make him a dead man and keep *all* the reward money.

TWENTY-FOUR

When Clint heard about the stagecoach holdup that had taken place less than ten miles east of town and resulted in the deaths of three men, he dropped his plans for that day and went to find the driver.

"His name is Art Beeson," the manager of the stagcoach line said, "and he lives up on B Street about two blocks away. It's a little place with a rose garden out in front and a white picket fence with a hanging broken gate. You won't miss it."

"Thanks." Clint turned to leave. "I'm sorry about the guards. I hear they were shot down from ambush and didn't even know what hit them."

The manager's face twisted into bitterness. "It was the most cold-blooded murderin' I've ever seen. I tell you, Mr. Adams, if you could get that Harry Blackstone and his new gang to the gallows, I'd sure be buying you drinks at every saloon in town."

"I'll do it for nothing," Clint said, still finding it impossible to believe that he could have been wrong and that Blackstone had escaped through an upstairs window. And yet, like Andrew Underwood had admitted, he could not have watched every window at once when the fire started.

Clint did not need his descriptions to find Beeson's house, because there was a pretty fair crowd of curiosity-seekers gathered in the driver's yard. Clint noted a bunch of barefoot kids and guessed they belonged to Beeson and the thin, haggard-appearing woman sitting on the front porch.

"Art," Clint said, shouldering through the crowd, "you mind telling me what happened out there?"

"I already told the sheriff and everybody else, Mr. Adams," Beeson said, recognizing him, "but seein' as how it's you, I'll tell it all over again."

"Thanks," Clint said. "Right from the start."

"You mean from where I left up in Virginia City about five o'clock this morning?"

"No," Clint said, "you don't need to start that early. Start from where you first saw the outlaws."

Beeson told his story again, slowly and thoughtfully, and those who had heard it several times already seemed no less fascinated by the killings and how Blackstone himself had decided that Beeson could live.

"I guess he just took mercy on me," Beeson said quietly. "After killin' all the others, I thought sure that I was a dead man."

"Praise God for the man's mercy!" Beeson's wife cried, hugging a snivel-nosed toddler. "Praise Him, I say!"

"Amen," several men answered.

Clint took a deep breath. "So you're sure that you had a real good look at Blackstone?"

"Oh, yes sir! He was ridin' his horse not twenty yards from me. The rising sun was a little bright in my eyes, but you couldn't miss that black spade beard or his hair."

"He was hatless?"

"Yeah," Beeson answered. "Come to think of it, that is a little odd, isn't it? Guess maybe he lost his hat ridin' to ambush us."

"Maybe," Clint said, feeling his suspicions rise. "Did he in any way look familiar?"

"Hell no! I never saw Blackstone before and I never want to see him again!"

"Then how can you be so sure that it *was* him?"

"Well, because of the description I heard, of course. I saw the reward posters, too. It was him all right."

Clint had his strong doubts, but since he had no proof to back them up, he kept them to himself. "Thanks for your help."

"I told Blackstone I wouldn't tell anybody that it was him," Beeson said as Clint turned to leave. "And you know what?"

"What?"

"I almost had the feeling he thought that was kind of funny."

"Humm," Clint mused. "Doesn't make sense, does it?"

"None of it does," Beeson said quietly. "Them three guards were my friends. Jack, he was the one with the shotgun, and he died right in my arms."

Clint patted the man on the shoulder. "I'm real sorry about them, and I'll do everything I can to see that whoever did those killings hangs."

A barrel-chested man said, "What do you mean, 'whoever' did it! Art just told you that it was Harry Blackstone and his gang."

"Blackstone's gang died a few days ago in Reno, gunned down outside the Washoe Bank," Clint said.

"Then Blackstone hired himself some new guns."

"I wonder," Clint said. He again started to walk away, but then he stopped in his tracks and said, "Art, you said that the three guards died all in the same explosion of rifle fire, didn't you?"

"Yeah."

"And that Blackstone had only two riders with him, and they had rifles but he was holding a pistol."

"That's right. Why?"

"Just wondering out loud," Clint said. "It doesn't seem

likely that Blackstone would fire from ambush with a pistol. A man would be more inclined to use a rifle and shove it into his saddle boot before he rode out to demand your strongbox."

"I don't follow you."

"Did Blackstone have a carbine?"

Beeson's brow furrowed and he closed his eyes for a moment. "As a matter of fact, he didn't."

"Then my guess is that there was another rifleman who didn't show himself," Clint said.

"But why?"

Clint didn't answer, because he was already on his way to get his horse. He figured that he would have no trouble finding the site of the ambush, and then he'd measure the bootmarks of the man who'd hidden in the rocks. If the bootmarks were as large as Clint expected them to be, he'd have pretty damn solid proof that Big Joe Gritts had been the third ambusher. It was evidence enough to get an arrest warrant and brace the murdering giant.

He was in Doctor Olms's cluttered office a few minutes later.

"Why do I have to go out there with you?" Olms groused. "I'm no lawman."

"True, but you're the closest thing to a scientist, and I want you to take some measurements," Clint said. "And besides, you're the one man in Carson City who could testify that the bootmarks had to have been made by a giant and that they exactly match the boots of Big Joe Gritts."

"Just expect me to ask Gritts for them boots?" the doctor snapped with irritation. "Because I'll refuse."

Clint had to grin. "If we tangle, he'll die with those boots on, and then I'll have your testimony to support my suspicions."

The doctor wasn't happy, but he could see Clint's point of view. Olms had already inspected the bodies of the three guards so that he could issue the coroner's report, and what he'd seen had left him in a grim and nasty mood. "Then let's get this over with," he sighed.

It took them a little more than an hour to reach the ambush site. The signs in the dirt were plain enough for anyone to see, and even the doctor began to take an interest when Clint led him over to the rocks.

"Here's where they waited and, as you can plainly see, there are *four* sets of hoofprints."

"But no bootprints."

"Don't be so sure of that," Clint said, dismounting and handing his reins to the doctor. "Generally, if men have to wait more than five or ten minutes, they'll dismount, and I expect that we'll find tracks around her pretty quick."

Clint was right. About fifteen yards away, he saw a dark place on the ground where one of the men had taken a leak, and nearby there were plenty of bootprints. Clint dropped to his hands and knees and began to trace the ground.

"Just keep the horses back so they don't trample on our evidence," he told the doctor.

"It isn't going to stand up in a court of law," the doctor warned. "I can tell you that right now."

Clint smiled. "Maybe and maybe not, but it'll be enough to get me an arrest warrant from the judge if we both do some fast talking. And Gritts would rather die than be put behind bars again. I know that and so does he. Now, tie the horses up to some brush and come on over here with that ruler you brought."

The doctor grumbled a little but he did as he was told, and when he saw the bootprints that Clint pointed out, he was astonished. "My Lord! They're huge!"

"You've seen Gritts. His hands are as big around as plates. His feet are also immense. I'd bet my life that these are his and will measure out the same size."

The doctor measured them and whistled under his breath. "Astonishing! They are seventeen inches exactly!"

"Good," Clint said with satisfaction. "Then all we have to do is convince the judge that only one man in the entire state of Nevada has feet that big—Joe Gritts. Will you help me?"

The doctor studied Clint's burned face, and then he looked down at his ruler lying beside the extraordinary bootprint. The decision was easy enough.

"Judge Arnold and I play poker together every Friday night. I'm a better player than him and I've won a considerable amount of money over the years, but he'll still listen to me when it's important."

"Thanks," Clint said. He removed his black Stetson and placed it gently over the bootprint, then covered the brim with dirt. "Just in case we need to preserve the evidence," he explained.

"You don't miss a trick, do you?"

"Not when it comes to Joe Gritts and my life I don't," Clint said as he headed for the horses.

An hour later, they walked out of Judge Arnold's office with a warrant for Joe Gritts. The judge, a florid-faced and portly little man with white hair and brown eyes, looked troubled.

"I'd sure rather Sheriff Williamson carried out this arrest warrant than you, Mr. Adams. After all, that is his job."

"I know." Clint frowned, but then he smiled. "I tell you what, Judge. I'll just see that the sheriff tags along and makes that arrest. I'll back him up if he wavers."

"Oh, he'll waver plenty!" the judge said, his voice thick with contempt. "I've been trying to get someone to unseat him from office for years, but Williamson is real smart. Just before an election, he puts on quite a show."

"I've seen it before," Clint said. "No matter. We'll see how firm he is when he has to hand Gritts an arrest warrant."

Doctor Olms shook his head. "Now, that moment is one I will be damned sorry to miss out on," he said.

"Me too," the judge said. "But like I said about the boot measurement," he added, "it's not hard evidence. Someone could conceivably have manufactured some device to make it look like a bootprint.

"Not likely, Judge."

"I'm sorry," the judge said, "but to convict someone of murder, you have to have irrefutable evidence, and a print in the dirt just isn't enough."

Clint expelled a deep breath. "As long as Gritts doesn't know that, we're all right," he said as he headed for the sheriff's office.

TWENTY-FIVE

Sheriff Williamson glanced up at the clock on his wall. It was only noon, he thought, feeling his belly rumble with hunger. He'd already put in the longest day of his life. He'd been up long before daybreak and out in the saddle before first light, then the long wait in the rocks, and finally, the bloody ambush of the guards.

What the sheriff really felt like doing was getting drunk, but, of course, that was out of the question until after closing hours. He'd had a steady stream of people through his office all morning, demanding that something be done about the murdering Blackstone Gang.

Williamson leaned back in his office chair. Ten more minutes and he'd lock up the office and go eat. He'd have steak and potatoes, maybe a piece of apple pie, and then he'd smoke a damned good cigar and try to gather himself for a long afternoon. That night, he'd hole up in his shack, maybe invite a saloon girl he knew could use a few extra dollars, and lose himself in the liquor and the whore.

In a day or two, Big Joe Gritts would come riding in with the bodies of Hank and Ernie lashed across their horses. The whole town, of course, would come running, and then Art Beeson would identify them as members of the Blackstone Gang and there would be another four thousand dollars of reward money to split up.

It all sounded fine until he remembered that Gritts would kill him one day if he did not kill the giant first.

The sound of boots on the walk outside made the sheriff frown. It would be more city fathers demanding that he do something, anything, to quell the rising anger of the citizens of Carson City. Well, the sheriff thought, I'm about ready to tell the whole damn bunch of them to stuff their sheriff's badge up their asses sideways!

Williamson allowed himself a smile. By damned, he *would* tell them to go to hell! He was quitting!

The sheriff was just starting to unpin his badge when the Gunsmith came striding through the door.

"Off that fat butt of yours!" Clint yelled. "Judge Arnold just issued a warrant for the arrest of Joe Gritts and you're going to serve it."

"The hell you say! I'm quitting this job as of right now." To show that he was serious, Williamson tore the badge from his shirt and slammed it down on his cluttered desk.

Clint looked at the badge, and then he picked it up and clenched it in his fist. "Never thought I'd be making a man of your low caliber put a badge on, but I'm about to do it now."

"You can't force me to do that!"

"Watch me," Clint said, his hand fading toward his gun butt. "We can do this the hard way or the easy way. And you don't even want to do it the hard way, Sheriff."

Williamson's eyes bugged with fear but he blustered, "If you shoot me, you'll hang."

"I'm prepared to take that chance," Clint said. "There are no witnesses, and I've just talked to the judge. He doesn't seem very impressed with your character, and I think he'd let me off with a warning if I said I shot you in self-defense."

"I don't believe it!"

"You better," Clint said, "especially seeing as I have your

bootprints and those of Joe Gritts protected out by the ambush site."

"What!"

"You heard me," Clint said. "That's how I got the warrant."

"Let me see that!"

Clint handed the paper to the sheriff and reiterated how he'd left his hat to protect the evidence left by the sheriff and Gritts while they'd waited to ambush the stagecoach guards. By the time Clint was finished, Williamson had grown several shades paler.

"What's the matter?" Clint asked. "You don't look so good."

"Gritts will kill me," the man whispered.

"Naw," Clint said. "You just help me find him and serve the warrant, and then be prepared to back my play if I go down."

When Williamson didn't answer, Clint said, "Let's ride. I hear that Gritts has a cabin up in the Sierra foothills. Since you and him are such good friends, I have a hunch you'll help me find it."

The sheriff had already lost his appetite. Short of refusing and being gunned down by Adams, he could not refuse the man's order. That being the case, he got his hat and stepped outside.

Andrew Underwood and the half-breed girl galloped up to meet them. "Clint, we've been looking all over town for you," said Underwood.

"Excuse me a moment, Sheriff," Clint said as he slipped in between the two riders.

Veronica Valdez looked beautiful. She had new clothes and a fine, wide-brimmed hat to protect her skin from the sun. Her black hair was brushed to a shine, and the hardness he'd seen in the firelight up on Gold Hill was absent. She looked almost girlish and innocent.

"Thank you for saving my life, Mr. Adams," she said to him.

"It was a pleasure." Clint looked over at the sheriff, who was waiting impatiently, and then back at the girl. "They say that Harry Blackstone is still alive, but I know different."

"So do I," Veronica said. "He would not have jumped. That was not his way."

"Clint," asked Underwood, "what can we do to help?"

"Ride back the way you came."

"What!"

Clint pulled them together a little closer, and then he told them what he wanted.

Underwood looked skeptical. "Are you sure?"

"Yeah."

They exchanged glances, and Underwood said, "It might take days instead of hours. We'll need some blankets and food."

"That's right, but I got a feeling you'll enjoy the vigil."

Underwood and the girl both blushed. "We want to get married, and we thought that you and Miss Butler might—"

"Sure," Clint said. "But after this is over."

They nodded, and then the young couple rode away.

"What the hell was that all about?" the sheriff snapped when Clint returned to his side.

"Just personal business," he said. "Let's go find Mr. Gritts and make the arrest before it gets dark."

"He's got a big mongrel," the sheriff said. "We won't get within half a mile of his shack before that dog starts barking a warning."

"Then you'll have to go in alone and draw him out."

Williamson shook his head. "Not on your life. He's planning to kill me anyway. Reckon he'd do it now as soon as later."

"Not likely," Clint pointed out, "because he still needs you to help him claim the reward for the two men that he plans to turn in as members of the Blackstone Gang. Isn't that right?"

"Yeah, but—"

"Williamson," said Clint, "when the dust settles on this, you're going to either hang or go to prison for a long, long time. I guess you know that."

"I don't know nothing of the sort!"

Clint pretended not to hear the man. "If you cooperate on this, I'll recommend that you go to prison instead of the gallows."

"Bein' a lawman, I'd never last a week in the state pen. You know that."

"It's a tough bed you've made to lie in," Clint admitted, "but as long as there's life, there's hope. It's your choice: Help and go to prison, or swing."

Williamson's fists knotted and he choked back a sob. "I should never have gotten messed up with him!"

"You disgust the hell out of me," Clint said as he went for his horse. "Most despicable man alive is a lawman or a preacher gone rotten."

When he was in the saddle, Clint reached back into his saddlebags and pulled out a derringer, which he slipped into his shirt, just behind his belt. He checked his gun and glanced at the carbine in his saddle boot. He had a feeling that either he or Joe Gritts was not going to see sundown. One way or another, the last card of this murderous Nevada game was about to be played.

TWENTY-SIX

It was late afternoon when Clint and Williamson dismounted at the end of a windswept ridge. They hid their horses in the pines and then crept through some brush to a place where the sheriff pointed out a sagging log cabin about half a mile away.

"That's it," Williamson announced.

Clint's heart sank. Gritts had found a perfect vantage point, from which he had an unobstructed view of the entire trail leading up to his cabin, situated at the base of an old rockslide. The cabin was tilting downslope and had probably been pushed nearly off its foundations on several occasions. Clint noted that there weren't even any huge boulders to help a man sneak up on the cabin, and the slide had wiped out every nearby tree.

"There's the dog," Williamson said, pointing as a huge, wolflike beast came trotting into sight from around behind the corral, where three horses were penned. "And he's every bit as mean as he looks."

"I don't suppose Gritts brings him in for the night."

"Hell no!"

"Then there's no point in waiting for darkness," Clint said, resigning himself to the fact that he'd have to simply fight his way forward, hoping he got in a lucky and fatal shot before the giant.

"All right," Clint said, "I want you to go get your horse and ride up to that cabin as if you had something damned important to say."

The sheriff balked. "I don't trust him!"

"I told you he won't kill you before he gets a hold of the reward money. He needs your help for that."

"Yeah," Williamson finally said, "I guess that makes sense."

"Sure it does. Now go get your horse and ride up there. Get him out where I can lay my rifle sights on him, and then get out of my line of fire in a hurry."

"You sure as hell don't have to worry about that," the sheriff said, sliding back deeper into cover and then lighting out to get his horse.

Williamson made the decision before he reached his horse that he was getting the hell out of Nevada while the getting was good. That meant he wouldn't collect any more reward money, but the game was over and he'd done well up to this moment. A winner knew when it was time to fold his hand and cash in his chips, and Williamson figured himself for a winner. The only thing that might trip him up was his incriminating bootprints out east of Carson City, but once they were eliminated, Williamson figured he was free and clear.

"So long," he called as he untied his horse and hauled himself into the saddle. "I hope you kill each other."

A few yards away and hidden in the trees, Clint smiled as he watched the sheriff ride away. He was sure that Williamson would gallop straight out to the morning's ambush site and wipe out the tracks. Andrew Underwood and Veronica Valdez would, of course, be waiting to surprise him, and their testimony would undoubtedly put a noose around Williamson's crooked neck.

Clint went to his horse and extracted his Winchester from its saddle boot before he returned to study the mountain cabin. The dog had not spotted him yet, but it would soon. It looked like it was half wolf, and Clint had a sad feeling he'd have to shoot the beast to get near Gritts.

Clint waited a few minutes more until the sun had dropped behind the Sierras, so that it would no longer blaze straight into his eyes as he advanced on the cabin. The moment the eastern slope of the Sierras was draped in shadow, he stood up and levered a shell into the chamber of his rifle, then started forward.

The dog saw him first. With a roar and a low rumble in its throat, it came streaking down the trail, straight for Clint, with its teeth bared.

"Call him off!" Clint shouted.

Gritts jumped through the door of his cabin, holding a rifle that looked small enough to be a toy in his fists.

"Dog!" he shouted. "Dog!"

Clint threw the rifle to his shoulder and planted his sights dead square on the onrushing beast's black chest.

"Dog!" Gritts roared again as he put his forefingers to his mouth and unleashed a shrill whistle.

Clint was just about to squeeze his trigger when the dog reversed direction and went galloping back to its master. Clint sighed in relief, because he had no quarrel with an animal trained to protect its master. But then again, he wasn't about to allow himself to become the beast's latest meal.

"What do you want!" Gritts shouted.

"I want the bodies of the two men you plan on delivering for a phony reward! And I mean to take you to jail."

"When hell freezes over!"

Clint reached into his back pocket and yanked out the arrest warrant. "I have a warrant for your arrest. I've got evidence you ambushed the stagecoach guards. You're going to hang if we have to use a set of logging chains."

Gritts barked a laugh. "My dog will soon be gnawing on our bones! You want to arrest me, come on!"

Clint nodded with resignation. The talk, the arrest warrant, all of it had been smoke in the wind. Everything came down to the next few minutes and depended on who could put a rifle or pistol slug into the other man first.

Clint started walking up the steep, rocky trail. He was still at the edge of his effective rifle range. Gritts, however, must have thought differently, because he knelt and balanced his elbow on one knee, took aim, and fired.

Clint swore as he felt the wind of the rifle slug whip past his ear. He kept walking forward, and his heart was booming in his chest as Gritts fired twice more, the third bullet plucking at Clint's jacket.

At last, Clint also dropped down to one knee and slowly squeezed off a shot. And missed. He was firing uphill and had overcompensated for the elevation. But he'd seen Gritts jerk back, and he knew that he'd come very close.

Clint adjusted for the elevation, and then both he and Gritts fired at the same instant. Clint felt a shiver of blasted rock slice his cheek, but Gritts staggered, and the rifle tumbled from the giant's hands.

Clint stood up and started moving quickly toward Gritts, who seemed to totter like a town drunk. Clint could not see where the big man had been hit, but when he bent to pick up his rifle, Clint stopped, took aim, and fired again.

Joe Gritts seemed to rise up on his toes and then started backing toward the cabin. He was cursing and fumbling at his side, trying to grab and lift his sidearm. The huge dog sat down close to its master and howled.

Clint used one more bullet to bring Gritts down for keeps. The giant slumped to his knees and then pitched forward.

Clint shifted his rifle to his left hand and drew his Colt. When he came to stand over Gritts, he said, "Are you finished?"

Gritts didn't look up at him. "I knew you . . . you were

better'n me with a six-gun. But . . . but not a goddamn rifle!"

"Sorry to disappoint you," Clint said as he moved past the man and went into the cabin for the bodies of Hank and Ernie.

By the time Clint had the bodies tied across their saddles, Gritts was dead and the wolf-dog was howling at the stars.

Clint led the horses down to Duke, and then he mounted his black gelding and reined it around toward Carson City, with the dog's mournful howling strong in his ears.

They were waiting for him when he arrived: Lucinda, looking pale and frightened, Andrew Underwood and Veronica, and most everyone in Carson City.

"Where is Williamson?" Clint asked as he dismounted and took Lucinda in his arms.

"He's locked in his own jail," Underwood said. "We caught him dead to rights. He was about to rub out the tracks just like you said he would."

Clint nodded, feeling neither satisfaction nor regret.

Lucinda kissed his injured cheek. "There's something that they haven't told you yet," she whispered.

"If you mean that they're getting married, I know about that and couldn't be happier," Clint said.

"There's more," Underwood said, placing his hand on Clint's shoulder. "They found the stolen money buried under two feet of rock in Blackstone's basement. It's a little brown around the edges, but it'll spend just fine."

Clint really smiled then as he pulled Lucinda close to his chest. "If I don't watch out, I could wind up marrying a real wealthy lady."

"Is that a promise?" she asked.

"Nope," Clint said, choosing his next words carefully, "at best a cautious prediction."

Lucinda kissed him on the lips. "Come along to my house,"

she said. "I'm going to see what I can do to make sure that your 'prediction' comes true."

Underwood's eyebrows shot up, and even Veronica was surprised by this boldness in Carson City's most respected and wealthy young lady. But Clint wasn't surprised. And that night, he was going to sleep with Lucinda, but maybe the next day or one day soon, he'd ride on.

Watch for
TOMBSTONE AT LITTLE HORN
108th novel in the exciting
GUNSMITH series
from Jove

Coming in December!

J.R. ROBERTS
THE
GUNSMITH

___ THE GUNSMITH #94: THE STAGECOACH THIEVES	0-515-10156-7/$2.95	
___ THE GUNSMITH #96: DEAD MAN'S JURY	0-515-10195-8/$2.95	
___ THE GUNSMITH #97: HANDS OF THE STRANGLER	0-515-10215-6/$2.95	
___ THE GUNSMITH #100: RIDE FOR REVENGE	0-515-10288-1/$2.95	
___ THE GUNSMITH #102: TRAIL OF THE ASSASSIN	0-515-10336-5/$2.95	
___ THE GUNSMITH #103: SHOOT-OUT AT CROSSFORK	0-515-10354-3/$2.95	
___ THE GUNSMITH #104: BUCKSKIN'S TRAIL	0-515-10387-X/$2.95	
___ THE GUNSMITH #105: HELLDORADO	0-515-10403-5/$2.95	
___ THE GUNSMITH #106: THE HANGING JUDGE	0-515-10428-0/$2.95	
___ THE GUNSMITH #107: THE BOUNTY HUNTER	0-515-10447-7/$2.95	
___ THE GUNSMITH #108: TOMBSTONE AT LITTLE HORN (Dec. '90)	0-515-10474-4/$2.95	
___ THE GUNSMITH #109: KILLER'S RACE (Jan. '91)	0-515-10496-5/$2.95	
___ THE GUNSMITH #110: WYOMING RANGE WAR (Feb. '91)	0-515-10514-7/$2.95	